SPUR #13

RED ROCK REDHEAD

DIRK FLETCHER

LEISURE BOOKS NEW YORK CITY

A LEISURE BOOK®

June 2004

Published by

Dorchester Publishing Co., Inc.
200 Madison Avenue
New York, NY 10016

ISBN 0-8439-2305-9

Printed in the United States of America.

Visit us on the web at www.dorchesterpub.com.

RED ROCK REDHEAD

ONE

"We're gonna kill us some Navajos," the tall, black-haired, piercing-eyed man said to his partner. They'd halted their horses in the shade of a scarlet rock formation that blotted out the Arizona sun.

Michael Stanton looked at his companion. "Don't you feel it? I think we'll find us some renegades, or some Indians that can't seem to stay on the reservation." He paused and grinned. "Hell, I hope so. We need to keep in practice. A tin can on a fence post is okay as a target, but nothing'll beat a moving, breathing redman." Stanton laughed, nudged his horse closer to his friend's, and slapped the man's back. "Colby, let's find us some red flesh."

Dave Colby grinned. "Sure. That's what I'm waiting for!"

He turned his gaze away, allowing Stanton to study the man. Colby was wiry, the opened buttons of his muslin shirt showing a lean and powerful frame. His clean-shaven face was angular, harsh, with red-streaked eyes and a nervous mouth. His face was caked with dusty sweat.

"Where do you wanna go?" Colby asked, staring at the horizon.

"There," he said, pointing to a clear area next to Echo Creek Navajo Reservation.

They rode out from the shade into the powerful Arizona sun. Though the rocks area was high desert, the temperature was over ninety.

Gotta find me an Indian, Stanton thought. Gotta do my good deed for the day.

Cottonwood Creek trickled beside the old Indian who lay on his back, eyes closed to the sky. The man's arms had been painstakingly tied to his torso, and his hair carefully knotted on his head for the journey. His body was fastened to a land sled made of a skin stretched over a wooden frame.

He'd have been buried by now if they hadn't decided to make this trip, Willow Woman thought as she looked at the dead man. She was a short, rather attractive Navajo, with rich black hair and tired eyes. Her face was fleshy but her body tight and trim. She dressed in bright cotton skirts and a blouse in white woman's fashion.

As she glanced at her husband, Willow Woman sighed and pitied him. She hadn't realized the effect his father's death would have on the otherwise strong man, nor the extent of his illness.

"You're tired," she said, walking to him. "We'll rest for a while longer."

"No!" Rising Cloud said, gesturing forcefully. "I'm not sick. We go!" He nodded toward his dead sire. "Father must be buried in sacred ground. I won't allow the round eyes to take away our spirit world like they've taken away everything else! He must be buried in sacred ground!"

Rising Cloud was dressed in a soft leather breechcloth, tan leggings and moccasins. His normally powerful chest was sunken with disease,

8

the once proud face now showed pain.

"There are new sacred grounds," Willow said quietly. "The shamans have said so. There's bell mountain and the thornapple grove, and—"

"Still your tongue!" Rising Cloud shouted, then stared at her in horror. "Others may not care where their ancesters go, but my father will not be buried on the reservation! We've walked half a day; it's too late to turn back."

"I know," she said. "All I meant was that you looked tired."

He coughed, then, and Willow shut her eyes against the gurgling sound in his chest. He had the cough, she thought simply. Within a few months he'd be dead. Another *gift* from the white man.

Cloud bent at the waist, loosening mucous and hacking it out on the ground. As was custom, he quickly covered the spot over with sand to ensure that no one used his spittle in the eagle pit way witchcraft, to make his body rot away.

Willow saw the superstitious act and smiled, but covered her mouth before her husband could take offense. He lived in the past. The white men were here and they've taken our lands, our ways of life, cut in half our strength in numbers, Willow thought. Rising Cloud couldn't accept that.

A cry from behind them spun Willow's head to the creek. Her two year old son, his naked light brown skin glowing in the full sunlight bouncing off the red sand, sat down hard and held up his foot.

Rushing to him, Willow saw the cactus thorn in his big toe. With a kind word she gently removed the barb from the boy's flesh, who sent up a louder roar.

"Quiet, Smooth Pebble!" Rising Cloud said,

exploding at his son. He walked to him. "You'll scare away your ancestors' ghost! Still your tongue!"

The boy howled again and Willow took him in her arms, cuddled and kissed him, turning her back to her raging husband.

Rising Cloud walked off to inspect his bow, then suddenly began gathering their few travelling goods. "We leave. Now!" His voice was cold.

He's pushing himself too far, Willow thought as she strapped Smooth Pebble to her back and lifted the skin-wrapped bundles. She waited for Rising Cloud to hook the rope loop around his waist, lift the land sled and walk forward, dragging his father behind him.

The baby squirmed on her back, so Willow stilled the child with a gentle hand. Her husband was dying, she thought again, without emotion. She should have left him months ago. Now, it was almost too late. Willow couldn't leave a dying man.

She was sad—why couldn't Rising Cloud have a woman who loved him during his last few months?

They walked on through the valley, the awesome red rocks jutting vertically above them in magnificent contrast to the blue sky and spots of dark green chapparel vegetation. She did not walk behind her husband as was customary, for she couldn't follow a dead man—his spirit might take offense. Instead, she stayed to Rising Cloud's right. The crunch of their moccasins on the dry ground was silenced by the heavy scrapings of the death sledge.

As she stared at her husband, Rising Cloud's head suddenly cocked to the right. He stopped and motioned her to do so too, his face tense with effort. Rising Cloud moved his head a bit further to follow the sound.

"Riders," he said, glancing around the area. No cover for miles in all directions. "Come. We go for the trees." He stumbled off, dragging the land sled.

The old man's body bumped off rocks and clumps of dry-leaved plants as they hurried toward the distant trees. Willow Woman didn't look back out of fear or curiosity. She had no time to fear, and if white men were approaching she had no time at all.

They were off the reservation; even though they were clearly on a ceremonial journey she had no doubt that any white man who saw them would rob them and, perhaps, kill them.

Too many Navajo had died lately while they were away from Echo Creek. Too many, Willow Woman thought again, glancing at the stand of trees.

She broke into a run, sliding the baby to her bosom where she held it tight. Passing her husband she continued on, blindly dashing for the too distant trees, images of her son's bullet pierced chest flashing by. Her husband was nearly dead; her father was dead; but her son must not die!

"Willow!" Cloud called out from behind her.

She glanced over her shoulder at him. "What?"

Cloud halted, his wheeze audible from fifty feet. His shoulders slumped and the normally handsome face was twisted with pain. Coughs boiled out of him as Rising Cloud's chest convulsed.

She hesitated, stopped, turned to her husband out of concern and some vestiges of love, then looked to the trees and the safety them promised.

"Willow!" he shouted again. "Go on! Run for the trees! Take Smooth Pebble with you but leave me here!" His words dissolved into hacks.

The baby gyrated on her chest, struggling to move down to suckle. Willow Woman, shocked at her husband's lack of concern for himself, dropped the bundles and rushed to him.

"How far are they?" she asked, touching his back.

His voice scratched out of his throat. "Four minutes."

"Then it doesn't—never mind." She shook her head forcefully. Even though they might not make it to safety they had to try. She straightened up her husband. "Come. We'll go to the trees."

"Willow, I said—"

"No! Come!"

He reluctantly lifted the loop to his waist and, bending from the sledge, moved toward safety, Willow Woman urging him along with her grip on his right arm. Rising Cloud held the thick rope that bit into his stomach, then pushed it down toward his groin so that the bumping didn't disturb his lungs. He continued to cough and spit diseased mucous, but he did not cover it. No eagle pit way magic was needed for Rising Cloud, Willow thought.

Though her ears were keen, Willow Woman heard no riders approaching, and hadn't before the sled cut up the desert's silence. Maybe her husband had been wrong. Perhaps he'd only thought he'd heard it.

Cloud grunted as he struggled to pull the heavy sled over a mass of rocks. He rose to the balls of his feet, straining, and the rope snapped. Rising Cloud fell three feet onto his face, shouting as his flesh banged against myriad sharp rocks and cactus spines. As he rolled onto his back, spots of blood broke out on his chiseled chest and flat stomach.

The coughs continued as Willow Woman bent over him.

"Willow—" he said, and his face twisted with pain. He reached for her and touched her shoulder. "I am dying."

"No," she said. "Your throat is dusty from the journey."

Cloud looked at her sadly. "You know I am dying. You've been telling me for weeks that I've been sick. I've known."

Willow dabbed at the spots of blood on his skin, trying to remove them with her fingers. It pained her to see her powerful, brave husband lying on his back, giving up.

"Before I die I must move my father's body to the old site. I must!" he roared.

Willow Woman gasped to see the old fire in his eyes, the fierce expression.

"But I don't know that I'll make it to the old lands."

"Maybe the whites won't find us," Willow said.

"Even if they don't, the cough has already found me. It wraps around me like a snake." He shook his head and coughed again. "Promise me, Willow, one thing."

She smiled down at him and cradled his head in her hands. "Of course."

He closed his eyes. "Take my father to the burial grounds, to the old sacred places."

Willow's lips trembled. She hesitated. But what did it matter? They'd both be dead anyway. "I will."

Rising Cloud smiled faintly, his lips trembling.

"I knew you would."

Willow knew she couldn't drag the land sled and hoped that Rising Cloud wouldn't think of that. Now that it was quiet again she could hear the horses approaching, but didn't look up to see them.

"They're coming," he said.

"I know."

"You must take Smooth Pebble and leave this place."

"No." Willow Woman looked into his eyes. "I won't leave you."

"Then you die because of me. I kill you, then."

"No!" she said.

"Yes. You stay for love for me. You should go for love of Smooth Pebble."

She stroked the baby's fine black hair unconsciously. She couldn't leave him yet, not while he was still alive. Even though she had the baby, she couldn't leave him.

"If I go they will surely follow me. No. I would rather stay here with you, Rising Cloud. You are my husband, but I will not leave you here."

"Then I will beat you for disobedience," he said, managing a shaky smile.

Willow Woman smiled too, even as she heard the quick approach of the horsemen. She wouldn't look up to see their dust trail, nor the horses themselves as they neared. A minute later they stopped twenty feet away.

"Hey, redman, you lazy, lying on your back that way?" one white man's voice said.

Willow didn't understand the words, but she looked up anyway. They were ugly; one taller man with hair on his face, and both smelled so bad she didn't want them to come closer. Neither held weapons.

"What you doing so far from the reservation? Going to the family burial plot, or out to buy whiskey?"

"Leave us," Rising Cloud said in English.

"The shit we will!" the hairy one said. "You know you ain't allowed off the reservation."

Willow Woman understood enough of that to respond.

"We bury. We go back. Now."

The taller man whipped up the rifle that had been slung across his knees and cocked it. "You ain't going nowhere, heathens!"

Rising Cloud sat and tried to stand, but fell.

The shorter man laughed. "Christ, looka that. The goddamned Indian's drunk!"

Why don't they just kill us, Willow Woman wondered.

As if in answer, the clean-faced man's rifle barked and Rising Cloud fell backwards onto the sand, his face composed, one last cough escaping before his lungs permanently emptied themselves.

Willow Woman didn't scream, but she clutched the baby to her breast.

"Don't worry, little lady," the hairy faced man said. "We ain't gonna hurt you—yet!"

She thought she understood. They weren't going to shoot her. Willow glanced at her dead husband and sobbed unexpectedly, emotion ripping her apart as she looked at the blue-black puckered hole in his chest. The baby struggled against her tight grip and cried out.

"Get rid of the kid and lay on your back, squaw," the hairy man said.

She didn't understand and shook her head. "*Como?*"

The men dismounted, watching her. The fuzzy

15

one walked up to her, slapped her face, and grabbed the baby from her arms. It yelled and kicked at the sight and touch of the strange man. He set it gently on the ground, then turned back to Willow. Backhanding her face once again, he reached down and ripped apart the flimsy cotton blouse. It fell away and her big-nippled breasts shone in the sun. He reduced her skirt to ribbons too and tore it from her body. She stood naked before them.

The smooth faced man pointed to the ground. Willow Woman killed off her emotions as she laid down and spread her legs. If only they wouldn't hurt the baby, she thought, she'd do anything.

A sharp word from the man made her look up at him. He stared between her splayed legs and grabbed his crotch, giving it a squeeze, then hurried out of his pants.

"Come on, Colby; we ain't got all day."

"I know. I'm hurrying."

He pushed down his drawers. His ugly white and pink penis reared up in full erection.

Willow Woman fought the urge to vomit and she laid her head back, staring at the small clouds that moved overhead.

Soon she felt his hard body on top of hers, the smelly white man's tongue shoving into her mouth and his penis jabbing painfully at her hole. She bit his tongue.

The man slapped her savagely. "Bitch squaw!" he said, then lifted her buttocks from the ground and forced himself into her, ramming as hard as he could. She cried out until the fuzzy man silenced her with his own massive organ.

A few minutes later it was over. She lay on her back, dirty, disgusted, her dead husband sprawled

16

nearby. The men, who had been talking, grew quiet and she heard the cock of a rifle. Willow Woman looked up in time to see the clean shaven man aim at her baby.

She screamed and scrambled toward him. The man turned his rifle and blasted a hole through her brain. Willow Woman dropped to the ground, her body shaking as it accepted another bullet.

She didn't hear Smooth Pebble scream his way into the spirit world.

TWO

In his Phoenix hotel room at first light Spur McCoy checked over his rations: coffee, biscuits, a can of peaches, bacon, a flask of whiskey, coffee beans, pemmican and jerky. Should last. Two freshly filled canteens, a metal cup and plate, coffee pot and skillet made up his mess. There was plenty of fresh water available every few miles or so. When he got hungry, he could knock down cones and feast on pine nuts once he reached the timber country. Like the Indians.

Spur remembered the telegram he'd received two days ago. General Halleck directed him to Hanging Rocks, Arizona Territory—a town four days ride due North from Phoenix, or longer during July and August, when the low desert's temperatures had fried more than one traveller.

Some Navajos had killed two ranching families; apparently the Indians had been gathered onto the nearby Echo Creek Reservation hadn't been quieted yet. This was the first such incident in years. Spur's job was to find the Indians responsible and also to try to convince the Navajo that their warring days were over.

He's known some Navajo in his travels, and had

19

lived with a group for a month. He couldn't speak
their language, but knew a few words. Some
Navajo had learned a little Spanish and English.
Communication would be difficult but manage-
able.

After looking over his bags, he packed everything, checked the Colt .45 in his holster, looked
over the Winchester, and set out from his hotel room
down to the front desk. An impatient ringing on
the bell brought the harried hotel owner's appearance. Spur paid his bill and was soon out in the
penetrating sun. He strapped on the saddle bags
and rose to the horse's back, then directed his
black and white stallion north out of town.

Spur was glad to leave the town behind him; as
civilized as Spur may have been, he wasn't a man
who had to have cities and people around him. In
fact, McCoy was happiest when he was alone with
a horse in the middle of nowhere. When he lay
awake at night on a soft bed he often wished he
was stretched out on a rough saddle blanket, his
coat spread over him and his head propped on his
saddle, smelling smoke from the fire and the taste
of fresh coffee in his mouth. He'd remember laying
his head back and watching the stars wheel above
him, with only an owl's cry breaking the stillness.
At such times he felt at peace and, generally, much
safer than in hotel rooms.

Spur's happiest day was when he was appointed
in charge of federal law enforcement west of the
Mississippi as a U.S. Secret Service agent. Now his
very job kept him travelling, seeing new places.

Spur McCoy was thirty-two, an inch or so over
six feet tall, with two hundred muscled pounds.
Confident eyes looked out from a face unlined with
worry or fatigue. Spur had brownish red hair, a full

moustache and mutton chop sideburns. He was dressed for the road—stained denim jeans, a light brown cotton shirt, Stetson, Colt .45 slung on his right hip and solid boots.

Certainly his father, a well-known merchant in New York City, hadn't planned for his son to grow up to become a Secret Service man. After graduating from Harvard, Spur worked in his father's business for two years, then with the start of the Civil War he embarked on a military career with a commission as second lieutenant.

He advanced in the infantry to the rank of captain before he resigned. Soon afterward he was called to Washington to be senior aide to New York Senator Arthur B. Walton, a long-standing friend to the McCoy family.

When the Secret Service Act was passed in 1865, Spur wangled an appointment as one of its first agents. After serving six months in Washington, Spur was transferred to the St. Louis office to handle federal law enforcement for the entire west. Spur was chosen for his marksmanship and riding abilities. He couldn't have been more pleased.

Now on his way to Hanging Rocks, a town he'd never heard of, Spur stared at the monotonous sand that stretched out around him, broken only by mesas and stands of giant sagauro cactus. He didn't relish four day's ride through the hot desert, but it was his assignment. At least it wasn't summer—two months from now the temperature could be twenty degrees higher.

A half hour later Spur saw a body lying on the ground before him. A horse stood nearby, nudging its apparently fallen rider. Spur trotted his mount to the spot, slipped to the ground and bent over the victim—a woman, Spur was startled to see.

Was she dead? He stared at her expressionless face and loosely closed eyelids. Dead or knocked out. He placed his ear against her chest and heard the soft pounding of her heart. The warm flesh below his head moved and pulsed.

She drowsily murmured something, and finally opened her eyes. When she saw Spur she smiled, then her face tensed and she wrenched away from him.

"Who are you?" she asked in a low voice, her eyes narrow with suspicion.

"Spur McCoy. I saw that you'd fallen from your horse. I was just seeing if you were dead or alive."

"I'm alive, thanks," the woman said, then winced and touched the side of her head as she sat up. She shook it and rubbed her eyes.

"Looks like you got knocked out."

"Damn him!" she said, looking at her horse. "He used to be so gentle. Something spooked him, I guess. He just threw me."

The woman was dressed in an ankle length leather skirt, high topped boots, and a doeskin fringed blouse. A dark brown hat lay nearby.

"You weren't using a saddle?" Spur asked, looking around for it.

"Of course, it's right—" She turned her head and frowned at the horse. "Where the hell did it go?"

"Could have been stolen," Spur suggested.

"If that happened I'm surprised the thief didn't take something else too." She smiled and started to rise.

Spur took her hand and helped her to her feet. "Are you sure you're all right, Mrs. . . . ."

"It's Miss. Bonnie Smith." She dusted off her clothing. "And yes, I'm sure I'm fine. I get thrown all the time. Some of these horses have a habit of turning on me. I don't know why; I'm a darned good horsewoman."

"You live around here?" Spur asked.

"Yes. About five miles south. My father's ranch."

Spur sensed that she was lying. "Do you mind my asking what you were doing out here all alone?"

Her eyes flared automatically, then she broke into a smile. "Not at all. I was out checking the fences," she said evenly, then crossed her arms.

Spur searched the area. There wasn't a fence for miles. "I see. Now, why don't you tell me what you're really doing, and where you were going, Miss Smith?" He gently gripped her arm.

"Let go of me!" she said, angry. He did so.

"Sorry."

"All right." Bonnie rubbed her wrists. "If you want the truth, I work in a saloon in Phoenix."

Spur smiled. He should have recognized the signs. She was a fancy lady.

"I was just going to make a—well, a house call. A man who lives on a worked out mine about five miles from here. He used to come to town, but he's getting old, so he pays extra and I borrow a horse and come out to see him regular. Every other Sunday." She looked at him defiantly as she placed her hands on her hips, the wind mussing her rich black hair around her head.

"That sounds more likely," Spur said, smiling. "Have you seen him yet?"

"No. I was on my way there—my god; what time is it?"

Spur pulled the Waterbury watch from his pocket on its leather thong. "Almost seven. You must have left early this morning."

"Damn!" she said. "I'm supposed to *be* there at seven, before he wakes up."

"I don't understand," Spur said. The woman was attractive, he had to admit—with a fresh, open face, exciting eyes, fluttering lashes and a quick, earthy smile that showed her worldliness. No blushing maiden, this one, Spur thought. He could only guess at the body beneath the rough riding clothes—but he imagined that it was exquisite.

"No, I wouldn't expect you to understand," Bonnie said, laughing. "The man has me pretend I'm a wild woman. I'm supposed to sneak into his house before he wakes up, hold a knife to his throat, and make him eat me out." She smiled, then laughed. "Hell, there are harder ways to make five dollars."

"That's all?" Spur asked. "I mean, that's all he does to you?"

Bonnie nodded. "I just sit on his face and squeeze my legs around his head." She smiled wider, and her tongue touched her top lip. "Has anyone ever told you you weren't too hard on the eyes, Mister—what did you say your name was?"

"McCoy. Spur McCoy."

"Mister McCoy." She moved to him and, after closely examining the bulge between his legs, reached out and gripped his groin, then massaged it with her fingers.

Spur didn't complain and soon felt his erection growing under her ministrations.

"Come on, Spur. Let's do it. You and me. Shit, the old codger's awake by now so I might as well have some fun. He doesn't want to see me now."

"What the hell," Spur said. "Sure. You can start by taking it out."

She knelt before him and unbuckled his belt,

24

then pulled his fly free of the five buttons. She pushed his jeans down and then his underdrawers. Spur's penis swung out like a stick.

"Christ, Spur! Nobody's seen more pricks than me, and that's a fine looking one!" She whistled and laughed. "You must've fertilized it to make it grow so big. I can barely get my hand around it!"

"Try getting your lips around it," Spur suggested in a hoarse voice. The unexpected sex had aroused him tremendously. His penis jerked in her hand.

"Sounds like a tasty idea to me!" Bonnie opened her lips and voraciously sucked his huge penis into her throat.

Spur's knees buckled when she hit home. The woman certainly knew what she was doing. He had to admit—virgins were fun, but there was nothing like an experienced woman.

"Yeah!" Spur said, turning his face to the sky, feeling the sun pound against his face while she mouthed him. "Christ, your throat's so hot!"

Bonnie moaned in answer and chewed gently on his penis. She suddenly grabbed his balls and squeezed, then pulled them gently away from his body, sending Spur into paroxysms of sexual fever. She simultaneously released his testicles and slid her mouth off his organ. Spur shuddered.

"Jesus Christ, Spur! You've got a man-sized prick!" She stroked its glistening length lovingly. "That's a real jaw breaker." Bonnie looked up at him guardedly for a moment, then smiled. "You know I'm no lady, McCoy, and you're certainly not acting like a proper gentleman right now, so I hope you won't be shocked if I say this."

He was intrigued. "Say what?"

She continued to masturbate him, keeping him

25

in full erection while she talked.

"I want you to ram this thing up my arse! Do it to me dirty, like the dogs!" Bonnie gave a sharp jerk.

"Hey!" Spur said, and brushed her hand away. "You won't get it anywhere if you treat it like that!"

"Come on," she said. "Stick it in!" Bonnie turned around and spread her legs, bent at the waist and planted her hands on the sand. She was opened to him.

Spur's breath came in ragged gasps as he knelt between her spread legs. He spat on his hand, rubbed the saliva onto his penis, then held his breath as he guided himself up into her tight orifice.

Bonnie yelled and beat the ground with her fists, arching her back and pushing toward Spur's thrusts. She sighed rhythmically in time with his grunts, tossing her head up and then swinging it down, bucking like a wild horse.

Bonnie dropped to one shoulder and reached down between her legs. Her thumb found her clit and she rubbed it vigorously, gasping as Spur continued to slid into her hot tightness.

"Yes, Spur!" she cried out.

He stared down in fascination, watching where they were joined. Spur's mind seemed to explode with sensation and he felt he could fly. His thrusts became shorter, almost spastic as he felt himself edge closer to ecstasy.

Spur dug his fingers into Bonnie's buttocks and felt his body ripple with power as she screamed and they climaxed together.

His hips jerked twice more, then he pushed his entire length into her and bent to press his chest against her back, his hands wrapping around to cup her breasts.

Later, Bonnie led Spur to a nearby stream, where they splashed like kids and washed themselves, then laid on a huge sloping rock at the water's edge to dry. Spur turned onto his back and pushed his cheek against the warm surface. He dozed, then woke when he heard Bonnie moving beside him.

Spur looked back and saw the woman admiring his body. She laid a hand on his right thigh and squeezed it, then ran it up and slapped his butt.

"You sure were better than that dried-up old miner," she said. "Hell, he never makes me come and can't even get it hard!"

Spur laughed and rose.

"Again, Spur? One more time? Except this time here?" She pushed a finger into her vagina.

"Sure." Spur smiled and she stretched out on the rock beside him. After a bit of positioning Spur pushed into her liquid hole, so different from where he'd just been.

They writhed together on the hot rock, Bonnie's legs crossing and uncrossing while she clutched Spur's torso. He pounded into her for five minutes and finally drove them both to paradise.

They uncoupled, dressed and returned to their horses.

"Where you headed?" she asked, buttoning up her boots as she sat on the ground.

"Hanging Rocks."

She looked at him curiously. "Really? Not many people go up there. Not much to do."

"Have you been there?" Spur buttoned his fly.

She shook her head. "What's your business in Hanging Rocks—if you don't mind my asking."

Spur shrugged.

27

Bonnie laughed shortly. "I see. Whatever made you come here I'm sure glad of it—elsewise I probably never would have met you." She finished the last button and stood, then walked to him and circled his waist with her arms. "Thank you, Spur McCoy. Christ, you fucked me to heaven and back."

"My pleaure." He kissed her quickly on the lips.

She didn't turn away or try to twist out of his grasp as their lips met.

THREE

Two days later Spur lay awake beside a sagauro, his stallion standing quietly ten feet away. The night was chilly and Spur had difficulty sleeping. He wrapped the blanket around him tighter and wished he'd brought heavier clothing.

The clear but thin sound of leather against sand pierced Spur's consciousness. He sat up and scanned the area but could see nothing save for the eerie outlines of the cactus trees and cottonwoods. A gibbous moon hung in a black sky, spilling scant light on the desert.

Spur detected no movement around him. If there were one or more men out there an investigatory search wouldn't do much of anything but hasten a confrontation—and they had the advantage. Besides, it was cold. Spur sat still, watching around him, but decided against looking for trouble.

After all, he might have been mistaken—he could have heard a brittle leaf moving against the sand, or a ripe prickly pear dropping. Spur listened for nearly a half hour. Nothing.

He shivered in the chill and finally slipped down onto his back, still wary and listening. Spur's

Winchester lay beside him on the ground; he was ready for anyone.

But soon Spur's head rolled to one side; his eyes half closed, lips parted. He dreamed until another sound explored in the still night. This time Spur grabbed the Winchester and jumped to his feet—only to see a ring of twelve Indians around him in the darkness, eyes gleaming in the moonlight. They were only ten feet from him.

The circle moved inward, the men never taking their aim off him—for they held bows with strings stretched back, Spur saw as they advanced. Two younger men had rifles. From their distinctive topknots Spur knew the men to be Navajos.

But they didn't look like reservation types—the Indians were dressed in leggings, breechcloths, hide coats. Spur looked for the eldest man; perhaps that would be their leader.

He held off firing to delay what appeared to be a no-win situation. The Indians moved closer until they stood shoulder to shoulder four feet from him.

"Friend," Spur said in Navajo.

The Indians murmured. One spoke aloud to the others. Spur didn't understand most of the words, but apparently the Indians were surprised at Spur's face.

Arrows were removed from bows, rifles lowered. Spur quickly set his rifle down.

"Friend," the old man repeated, in English.

What the hell was going on?

"We are sorry. We mean no harm."

"Happy to hear that," Spur said. "You speak English."

The man's lined face smiled. "Some English, some *Espanol*. The *padres*, the army . . . they teach."

30

"If you didn't want to hurt me why'd you sneak up on me like that?"

The man frowned. He was obviously piecing together a reply. "We thought you someone else. Bad white man. When we see face, we know you not him."

"Why do you want this man?" Spur asked, then looked at the ring of Indians who still stood rigidly around them.

The chief made a sign and the group broke up. They wandered off, sat in groups, waiting. Spur relaxed and sat across from the chief.

The elderly Navajo said something to a young man. Spur missed the words, but the boy quickly jumped up and disappeared, only to return momentarily with a pile of firewood which he quickly built blazing into a fire. He used a match to start it.

"You asked who we look for. We not know name. White man who kills *Dine,* Navajo. You could have been him."

"Where is this man from? Where does he live?"

The fire flickered crazily, casting strange shadows over the men. Spur didn't feel the slightest bit edgy about sitting with them, for he knew the Navajo were gentler than their kin, the Apache. As he looked around from face to face, smiling, Spur saw that the men were quiet, but restless. They didn't seem to want to be there.

But Spur knew the chief was a reasonable man; otherwise he'd be dead, along with a few of their number.

The man finally found words. "He lives Hanging Rocks, maybe." He peered at Spur across the fire. "Where you going?"

Spur frowned. "Hanging Rocks." McCoy decided to change the subject. "You say this man

31

kills Navajo?" He hadn't heard about it.

The chief nodded. "Yes. Ten of our people."

"From the reservation?" Spur asked cautiously.

"Reservation. Yes." He spat and moved sand with his moccasin toe to cover the liquid.

Spur knew that these Navajos were either runaways from the reservation or had simply slipped out for the night to track down the killer. It seemed strange that General Halleck's telegram hadn't mentioned any Indian deaths, just those of the white ranching families. If the whites had been killed out of retaliation for the Navajo deaths, the situation was much different.

"When did these killings take place?" Spur asked, eyeing the chief in the firelight.

"Some a moon ago; more yesterday. The white man was seen, not caught. Sometimes another man with him. We must find him." The chief's face was set. "We have been robbed of everything but our lives; now round eyes want those too."

Spur shook his head. "Not all of us."

The chief sighed. "I try believe," he said, shaking his head.

Spur decided he might as well take up a difficult subject. "Have you heard about the white families who were killed recently? Near Hanging Rocks?"

One young brave stood and looked anxiously at the chief, who motioned for him to sit. The man turned his head and spoke.

"Yes."

Spur was startled by the man's reaction. Had the Navajo killed the families? If so, were these men responsible? Spur inches his hand toward his holster that lay strapped to his thigh.

"Can you tell me anything about them?"

The Indian frowned. Spur wondered if he understood the question.

"I asked—" he began.

"I know what you ask!" the chief shouted. "Why
do you go to Hanging Rocks? Why?"

"I have to find out who killed the white
ranchers."

The chief smiled. "Government turn back on
Navajo, but when white killed, they send you."

Spur paused. How could the Indian have known
he worked for the government? Most of the men's
faces around the circle were tight, and a few angry.
The tension around the ground was palpable; Spur
could smell it.

"The government doesn't know about the
killings of your people," Spur said. "This is the
first I've heard of it, too."

The chief shook his head. "I not believe it. But it
not matter." He looked at Spur quizzically. "You
think we kill ranchers, my people kill them." He
had not asked a question.

"That's what the government thinks," Spur
admitted. "But I don't know that for a fact."

"Yes, government thinks that. Round eye
families killed, they say Navajo did it. Then more
Navajo die!" The chief made an unintelligible
gesture in the air. "Your people want us all dead.
Forgotten!"

"No. All I want to do is find the rancher's killers.
Who did it? Was it the Apache?"

The chief laughed. "No! *Estupido!* No Navajo,
no Apache!"

Spur was tiring of the old man's word games.
"Who killed them?"

His laughter died and he fixed his gaze on Spur's

forehead. "No Indians kill them. I sure of that. Was white man. Round eyes who made it look like Indians. When white tell another white Indian guilty, no questions. We are guilty!"

Several men whispered.

Spur instantly discounted the story, but remembered it. To smooth things over after the tense moment he decided to play along.

"White men, eh? If that's true, is it the same man you're looking for—the one who murders Navajo?"

"*Si*, yes, yes," the chief said hurriedly. "That what I tell you. We think he same man."

Spur frowned. The idea almost made sense, but Spur couldn't believe it. "We're looking for the same man," he said, not knowing what or who he was looking for.

The chief looked at Spur cunningly. "You not believe."

"I don't know what I believe," McCoy said quickly.

"I see it. But you will, round eye. You will know that white man killing Navajos and whites near Hanging Rocks. You see when you there."

"Maybe," Spur said.

The old man smiled. "Wind, moon, stars. All things shine, then pass. What happened between the *Dine* and whites, happened. Cannot be changed. Still, only want to be left in peace."

Spur didn't speak, but he believed the man. He didn't seem like the type to massacre the ranchers.

The chief rose suddenly. The others followed suit, as did Spur.

"We leave," the chief said. "You soon know truth." He turned and with his men behind him, disappeared into the darkness beyond the bright ring of light.

Spur, left alone beside the fire, was confused, disturbed by the meeting. If there was a white man killing Navajo around Hanging Rocks, it was possible he could have killed the ranchers too.

He shrugged and squatted before the fire, warmed his hands before it, then dumped dirt onto the flames until they were extinguished. No sense in attracting unwanted attention.

As soon as the fire was out Spur frowned. He could have boiled up some coffee first. Snarling, he laid down and stared at the stars above him. Soon the night closed down his mind, and all thoughts of the Navajo were far away as he slept.

FOUR

Caroline Stanton pulled the quilts over her head, pushing one ear into the bed and covering the other with her pillow in an attempt to block out the shouting. Always shouting, night after night. Wouldn't he ever stop?

As the noise finally abated Caroline pushed off the blankets and pillow and lay staring at the small, dark chandelier above her. At eighteen, she needed sleep too much to spend half her nights wide awake.

She ran a perfectly manicured hand through her blonde pincurls, a frown marring her otherwise lovely round face. Sometimes she wondered if her father was well. All these secret meetings, shouting matches really, Caroline thought; her father's strange behavior lately, guests at all hours of the night—he was doing something, but she didn't know what it was.

Because her father had built this two story palatial home out of red brick in Hanging Rocks, Caroline was spared hearing *what* was shouted, but rarely missed the muted booms.

Every time she tried to confront him with it, her father had talked her out of asking him. He might not have been aware of it, but that's what happened, she thought Tomorrow morning she wouldn't back down. Her father would explain everything to her.

Proud of her determination, Caroline rose and stepped into her slippers, then padded across the room. She knew she wouldn't sleep without some help, and so opened her huge oak wardrobe, pushed aside dozens of corsets, petticoats, dresses, jackets and other frilly delights, then reached into the far right hand corner. Her fingers grasped the metal bottle and pulled it from the closet.

She looked at it, opened the flask, held it above her lips and tipped it down. Full bodied red wine spilled into her mouth. She stopped the flow and wiped her lips as she swallowed, feeling the alcohol warming her stomach, then lifted the flask again. After three good slugs Caroline replaced the top, returned the bottle to the closet, and swung the doors shut.

Now comfortably full of liquid fire, Caroline laid in bed and closed her eyes. Even as her father began shouting downstairs again, Caroline dropped into a deep sleep as the wine seduced her.

"You fuckin' bastard!" Michael Stanton said. The tall, muscular man stood staring incredulously into another man's eyes inches from his. The second man stood a half foot shorter, and was backed against the door inside Stanton's private office at home. His fleshy face shone with sweat, the chin shaking.

"What the hell do you mean by that?" Stanton asked the man, who was dressed in a clerical collar.

"I mean simply . . ." the minister began. "What

38

I'm saying is that Indians—all men, of any color—have souls."

Stanton's brown eyes narrowed as he stepped back from the man. "You're shitting me, preacher man! That's insane talk! You know as well as I do that they're animals, savages."

"No," the minister said.

Stanton's face grew grim. "Are you saying no to me, Yasger?"

The man's face remained calm. "No. *God* is saying no to you."

"Fuck God!" Stanton blurted out, then turned from Yasger in a fury and stormed across the room to a mahogany bar. He poured a whiskey and downed it, then refilled the glass. As he turned back to the minister he started to leave. "Wait a minute, Yasger." His voice was calmer. "You really mean this?"

The man nodded shortly. "Of course. It's common sense. Anyone who thinks about it has to agree."

"Then you plan on preaching that come this Sunday? You think you should spread the word?"

The man's head bobbed again.

"I see." Stanton thought, tugging at the ends of his drooping straw-thick black moustache. "That means others might take that notion, too. And if that happens this town—this country—is in a shit-heap full of trouble." He stared at Yasger. "You're not going to spread that idea."

The man was stunned. "What did you say? Are you telling me—"

"Don't go spouting the idea that Indians got souls! That's heathen bullshit and you know it! Goddamn, our preacher's an Indian lover!" He

39

strode over to him. "Don't you know what those *souls* do? They're savages. These Navajo—they kill for pleasure. Not to eat, not to practice their hunting—for pure *pleasure!* And they mutilate their victims—cut off women's breasts, men's balls. I've seen it myself, not once but several times. They constantly break the treaties they signed with us of their own free will, and—"

"Mr. Stanton!"

"—wander off Echo Creek reservation to get drunk and rape white women! No, Reverend Yasger, you won't be telling the white folks to invite those savages into their hearts, homes and the kingdom of God! Do I make myself clear?"

The shorter man pounded his right hand, balled into a fist, against his left, but was silent.

Stanton laughed. "Good. I didn't think you'd argue with me. After all, I own you and your fuckin' church. As long as it makes a profit for me I'll let you run your god business. Just don't go spreading new ideas like that around here. Understand?"

Reverend Yasger nodded, lips tight and veined with white. He didn't meet Stanton's eyes and seemed ready to dash to the door.

"Good. Christ, Yasger, sometimes you take that Bible business too seriously. Just don't let it go to your head, okay boy?" He slapped Yasger's cheek with a cupped hand. "Now get the hell out of here. I've got things to do."

Yasger stared at Stanton with sad eyes and left the office without a word.

Stanton laughed and downed half the whiskey. That was a close one, he thought. Can't have any Indian lovers around here. No. Not now.

Stanton sat behind his desk and took out a

writing tablet and a pencil. He sat staring at the blank paper for ten minutes, not writing, and finally began jotting down names. When he had a list of twenty Stanton stopped and looked at the grandfather clock that ticked away in the corner near the window. Eleven P.M. Almost time.

He folded the paper, pushed it into his vest pocket, stood and removed the black coat from his chair and slipped it on, then walked from his office down the hall to the front door. He opened it an inch and paced on the polished wood floor, his boots clicking distinctively.

Everything was moving well so far. No problems, no leaks of information. The attacks on isolated Navajos had been one hundred percent successful. Public sentiment against them had been stirred up since the deaths of the ranching families a half month ago, and Sheriff Hughes was getting softer every day.

Stanton felt closer to his big dream, the one he'd carried with him for years, that had sustained him in rough times.

Rough times—Stanton felt the old bitterness flood through him as he remembered army life. A brilliant, promising career, he'd been told as a captain. Then that day when he'd gotten trigger happy while fighting some Cheyennes and shot at a man moving through the underbrush. A second later his lieutenant fell dead before him from the bushes.

Horrified, he managed to cover up the incident, telling the men that a Cheyenne had killed him. But the stress piled up on him. He broke down under fire and ran from the enemy—right into a court martial. Stanton had been lucky—he'd been given a dishonorable discharge and had his hands

41

slapped. But the shame that flooded through him every time he remembered that day when he'd turned and run hadn't diminished over the years. It still lived in his gut.

But Michael Stanton never made the same mistake twice. He had married and fathered a daughter while in the army, and he'd had to support them.

With penniless parents and no other living relatives or friends, Stanton moved his bride, Allyson and their three year old daughter, Caroline, to Hanging Rocks, a mining town near some of the richest gold veins in Arizona Territory. He had bypassed California and headed straight for Hanging Rocks, thereby beating out many other miners who, having failed in California, later drifted across the border into Arizona.

Within two years he had amassed nearly $100,000 through sheer luck and exhausting work. The mines he eventually owned continued to pay almost two decades later, not as well as they had in the beginning but profitably enough to keep them working. Stanton also owned several businesses and buildings in Hanging Rocks, which supplemented his income.

Now, sixteen years after his shame, he'd soon be back in an army—his own army! The beginnings, the men, only a few so far, would be arriving at any moment.

Stanton stood and walked to the hall just as the door opened. Dave Colby walked in.

"Where the hell have you been all night?" Stanton asked. "You disappeared after supper and we haven't seen your ass since."

"I've been fucking my brains out with Tillie," Colby said with a sheepish expression.

"That shouldn't have taken long." Stanton took a cigar from his vest pocket and lit it, then threw the match into a silver ashtray.

"Are they here?" Colby asked expectantly, his homely face, all angles and bones and stretched skin, still flushed from the athletic sex.

"No. It's still early."

Colby smiled. "Hey, are you going hunting tomorrow morning?"

"Maybe."

"Can I come with you?"

Stanton snarled. "We can't push the Navajo too far. Not yet."

"Why the fuck do you care how far you push them?" Colby asked.

Stanton smiled and puffed. "If they get organized, staged a real uprising, we would all care a damn lot!"

Colby snorted. "Shit, just seems like a good excuse to wipe them out."

"I know what I'm doing," Stanton said, his voice low and menacing. "Don't question me."

"I'm—sorry." Colby scratched his crotch. "Can I have a drink?"

"Of course." He waved toward his office.

Colby disappeared into it. As he did, the front door opened and two men walked in.

"Good evening, men. This way."

Stanton led them into the parlor, windows draped and two rows of chairs set up facing a podium. The men sat in the front row.

Within ten minutes half the chairs were filled. Stanton grinned as he stood in the rear of the building. At 11:21 he walked to the podium.

"Men, we're here to discuss my plans for a private militia for Hanging Rocks. Its only

43

purpose will be to eliminate the growing threat from the Navajos on the adjacent Echo Creek Reservation. We cannot sit idly by and watch our loved ones and friends being slaughtered by those savages!" Stanton's voice thundered in the room.

The men sat in rapt silence.

"We need a strong, organized, dependable fighting unit, composed of qualified men, preferably those with army experience. Any questions so far?"

None.

Stanton scowled. "Indians! God, how I'm sick of hearing that word! We've got to push the Navajos away from Hanging Rocks or we'll pay for our hesitation!"

"You mean move them away?" a gangly youth with no front teeth asked from the second row.

"We'll do whatever's necessary," Stanton said. "If that means wiping them out—killing them—we'll do it."

"The only good Indian's a dead Indian," a second called out.

Stanton smiled. "Damn right! That's the spirit, Buck! The way things are now it's either us or them—look what happened to the MacDonalds and the Goodnights! Massacred while they went about their daily business by those ungodly bastards! Are we going to let that happen to us?"

"No," one man shouted.

"Wait a minute," another said, standing.

"Shut up, Cousins," Buck, the man to his right, said.

"No! Stanton, are you saying we should kill every Indian? Are you trying to wipe out the Navajo?" Cousins stared at the man. "That's it, isn't it? You think you can murder—"

"It's not murder, asshole!" Stanton said, his

44

face flecked with red. "They're not human. Don't you know that? And yes, that's my plan. Why not?" Stanton's voice was tight. "Give me one good reason why we shouldn't wipe the Navajo off the face of the earth!"

"It's not right," Cousins said.

"Will you shut up?" the man next to him said.

"No, you shut your fuckin' trap, Buck!" Cousins said.

The room went silent. Stanton looked at the man, summed him up. "We're simply protecting ourselves and our families from the Navajo threat."

"Navajo threat! Bullshit, Stanton!" Cousins shook his head. "When you go out hunting Indians, just to kill them, you're not protecting anyone's ass. You're killing for killing's sake."

Stanton's temper flared again. He struggled to keep it under control. Mustn't let loose entirely before his men, he thought. Damn troublemaker, that Cousins. Buck never should have brought him. "If you feel that way, Cousins, then why the fuck are you here tonight?"

"I'm asking myself the same question. Hell, when Buck here told me about this militia I thought it'd be run by the government, or at least be a lawful assembly. This ain't nothing but a gang organized to wipe out the Navajos."

Stanton slammed his fist down on the podium, making it shake.

"You'll never see your militia, Stanton," Cousins said. "You'll never lead it into battle against the *enemy*." Cousins suddenly bolted toward the door. A second later he was out of the room. A bang echoed from the front of the house.

Stanton strode over to Colby, who stood off to

one side. "Get him," he said. "Slip out when it's not noticeable. *Kill him.*"

The man nodded, so Stanton returned to the podium. He looked at the riled-up men.

"This army, like any other, has rules. If you plan to join, you'll have to obey those rules." Stanton spoke in an unhurried voice as Colby walked from the room, attracting little attention. "Desertion is a violation of the regulations. Do I have to tell you the penalty for desertion?"

Stanton stared hard at Buck, who fidgeted in his chair. Colby left the room.

"On another subject, I told you men to be careful who you bring here. Didn't I?" He continued to stare at Buck.

"I—I didn't know Cousins thought like that," the thin faced man said, his hazel eyes shining with fear.

"Get the hell out of here," Stanton said. "I can't stand the sight of your face. Report back to me tomorrow; we'll talk then."

Buck rose and stepped from the room, not wanting to anger Stanton further.

"He never shoulda brought Cousins here," one man said. "I could have told him that."

"Just a few minor problems," Stanton said. "Some small ones. That's normal, so it's nothing to worry about. Things like this have a way of working themselves out."

Stanton spoke to the men further of his plans for the army. He mentioned the uniforms and arms he'd ordered, the camp they'd set up in the desert not far from Hanging Rocks, where the men would receive training.

"What about pay?" one man asked.

He smiled. Stanton realized he'd never mentioned the subject. "Rest assured you'll all be paid as soon as we're actually in training and fighting."

"How much?" another asked, a slouching fellow with a bald pate.

"Enough," Stanton said. "Just remember—your greatest reward will be seeing those redmen drop to the ground." He closed his eyes for a moment, remembering the Indians he'd killed and smiled. "That's enough pay for anyone."

FIVE

Colby's breath shot steam into the night as he hurried along Broad Street, glancing around the darkened town for Cousins. The man couldn't have gone far.

A flash of movement to his extreme right launched Colby into an all out run down an alley, his leather shoe souls slapping against the dirt and echoing between the buildings. No time for slow, quiet approaches. He had to silence Cousins.

The man wasn't in the alley, though, by the time he reached it so Colby continued down it, staring at the central patch of light at its end. He moved in near darkness, but knew instinctively that the alley was deserted.

Noises ahead made Colby increase his exertions. As he emerged from the alley Colby shot his head to the left, then right. A man walking, three hundred yards from him, turned a corner down Hogan Street. Colby cursed and headed toward it. The man was giving him exercise, he thought.

As he reached Hogan, Colby stopped. The man had vanished. He must have gone into one of the buildings.

Puzzled, Colby hurried around, searching for

Cousins. No sign of him. He looked at Cicily's Hotel, which stood directly in front of him, then recalled Buck saying his friend was staying at Cicily's. Room Ten, if he remembered right.

Colby walked leisurely across the street, though his body was tense, and he felt a tightness in his chest and stomach. He went in and, seeing no one in the lobby, walked up the stairs, turned right at the landing, and continued on to the last room on the left.

He didn't knock. Colby gripped the knob gently and tried to force it right or left. Something jingled but it didn't move. Locked.

Colby frowned. No way to open the door except to break it down. He backed across the hall eight feet, then dug in with his feet as he propelled his body. Colby smashed against the door, popping it off of its hinges.

The door fell into the room. Colby rushed in and saw Cousins turn around. The man stood stripped to his waist, a towel in one hand and a soapy basin behind him.

"What—what the hell do you want?" Cousins asked. He glanced at his gunbelt that hung on the brass bedpost three feet distant.

"It's over, Cousins," Colby said. He enjoyed watching the man squirm. "Stanton doesn't like troublemakers in his army."

"I never joined his army," the man said. "And I don't care what Stanton likes." He turned.

"Don't move," Colby warned.

"Hell; can't I splash these suds off my face?" he said. He spun quickly, hefted the half full basin and flung its contents in Colby's face.

Colby yelled and staggered back two feet, dropping his six-gun, the soapy water stinging his eyes, blinding him. "Where the hell are you, Cousins?" Colby yelled.

He heard the sound of footsteps as Cousins ran to the bed, got his holster and retrieved his weapon, a mother-of-pearl handled Colt .45.

"Now *I've* got the gun on *you*, Colby! Get the hell out of here!"

Colby sputtered and wiped water from his eyes with one hand. "No fucking way, Cousins!" He skimmed his cheeks and felt his eyes burn as he opened them. "You son of a bitch! That water's goddamned soapy!"

"Yeah. Now get your ass out of here!"

Colby saw the basin on the floor a yard from Cousins, directly before him. He savagely kicked it. The heavy porcelain basin banged into Cousin's legs.

The man looked down, cursing, as Colby drew his deady six-inch hunting knife from its sheath and then lunged foward as Cousins was distracted. He grabbed the man's right arm and slashed it with the knife until Cousins dropped the gun.

The stunned man jerked back out of the knife's reach. Colby grabbed Cousins' right hand and pulled the man forward, then plunged the knife into his stomach.

The blade ripped through the bare skin. Blood poured out and Cousins screamed hollowly as Coby dug the knife into his hot guts, twisting savagely, sending up another scream of pain.

Colby waited five seconds while Cousins frantically tried to break away from the man as he watched agony explode across his face. He then withdrew the knife and stabbed Cousins' left chest twice. Colby broke out into an itchy sweat as he labored over the killing.

Cousins' tense body finally went limp and he slumped to the floor, drool covering his chin, the eyes peaceful as fragments of intestine poked out from the stomach slash.

Colby, his breathing hard, bent to wipe the blade on Cousins' bare chest, pushed the knife into its sheath, stuck the man's Colt in his boot and holstered his own weapon, then left the room.

As he entered the hall he thought someone might have been brought by Cousins' cries, but it was empty. Colby sighed and rushed down the stairs, through the deserted lobby into the cool night air.

The sweat on his brow chilled as he turned left down the boardwalk to the Longbar Saloon.

"Hey, Colby!"

The voice was behind him. He turned and saw Buck standing a dozen feet from him.

"Meeting break up, Buck?" he asked, smiling, but as he approached the man Colby saw fear on his face.

"What were you doing in there?" he asked.

"In where?"

"Cicily's."

"Seeing a friend." Colby wondered if Buck guessed what he'd done. "Why?"

"Bullshit, Colby!" Buck said. "I know what you did! I heard what Stanton told you to do—kill him!"

Colby laughed and stepped forward, then used his fastest draw. The silver handled weapon flashed in the moonlight as the man swung it up and fired point-blank at Buck's chest.

The bullet struck the breastbone, shattering it and tearing the edge of the heart. It severed the spine and finally continued out the man's back.

Buck wobbled on shaky knees and paralysis

52

set in as Colby fired once more and fled into the shadows. The Longbar, a half block down, roared with music and laughter, shouting and an occasional scream of ecstasy from the upstairs rooms. Nobody could have noticed the shooting, Colby thought as he hurried toward Broad Street and the sanctuary Michael Stanton's home offered.

He hoped Stanton would have wanted Buck dead, but it didn't matter. It had come down to survival; him or me, Colby thought, and blinked as sweat trickled into his eyes.

Spur's stallion picked its way through rocky ground as he steadily approached Hanging Rocks. The area was mountainous, and the flat topped mesas of the lower desert were gone. In their place craggy, eroded red and brown ridges ringed the horizon on all sides. Some peaks rose closer, jutting from the four thousand foot high desert floor as if pushed there by some incredible subterranean force. Though small patches of green showed at the base of the cliffs, contrasting sharply with the volcanic, iron stained red soil, most of the cliffs were barren of trees, rocks hanging in the air; hence, the town's name.

Spur figured he wasn't more than an hour's ride from Hanging Rocks. In the distance he saw the tree enshrouded route of a creek or river, maybe Cottonwood creek, or Oak Creek. The land around him was rocky, covered with cacti and low chaparrel.

A few miles ahead, however, the land grew gentler. Cedar and pine trees shaded large areas, creeks snaked through, and ancient Indian irrigation canals still operated, crisscrossing the area with rivulets of sparkling water.

After his strange meeting with the Indians late last night Spur was impatient to start his work. The Navajo killings figured in somewhere, Spur felt. If the first Indians were killed four weeks ago, as the old chief had said, that meant that the killings hadn't happened until two weeks later—so the Navajo's apparent attack on the ranchers could indeed have been in retaliation. But why wait two weeks? And why those two families? Perhaps the ranchers were the ones responsible for the earliest Indian killings—after all, their spreads were much closer to Echo Creek reservation than Hanging Rocks. On the other hand they were easy Indian targets.

Spur shook his head and looked up at the blue-white sky. A hawk circled overhead in hypnotic arcs. To his right a dust devil whirled. It tugged at a Russian thistle's roots, lifted it from the ground and swirled it upward.

Half an hour later Spur tied up his horse before the only hotel in town, the Cicily, and registered in Room Ten—just one vacancy, the kindly matron had explained. It had opened up this morning, and the man had skipped town without paying. She hoped there wasn't a mess on the floor.

Spur didn't see anything wrong with the room when he went to it, chucked his bags, and headed for the sheriff's office. He was supposed to meet Vance Hughes.

The man turned out to be a homely, boyish sheriff, his face an orb of sallow flesh with hesitating eyes and a weak chin. Hughes dressed in denims and a pressed white shirt with a black string tie, his uncovered head largely bald. A claw-scar on his right cheek marked some early childhood confrontation with nature.

Hughes seemed introverted, soft spoken, Spur thought as he walked into the man's office, but able to be effective if he put his mind to it. He wondered if Hughes was the sheriff simply because no one else wanted the job.

"You must be McCoy," Hughes said, rising from his small oak desk.

"That's right," he said, surprised. "Vance Hughes?"

The sheriff nodded. "Glad you made it here so quick." A scant smile lit his face. "Ever since the army pulled out we've been open to things like this."

"Things like what?"

"Hell, the attacks on the MacDonalds and the Goodnights. I know some older folks who're afraid to go to sleep at night. Grandmother Martin is always seeing a redman peeking in when she dresses for bed."

"Have you heard about the Navajo being murdered around here recently?"

Hughes shook his head. "No, but I probably wouldn't either. What do we care for them? They ain't U.S. citizens."

Spur paused. "Indians are human beings. I've heard that ten were killed in the last month— some two days ago. Apparently some white man's shooting them down."

Hughes laughed. "What kind of story is that?" He looked at Spur. "Where'd you hear that?"

"None of your business."

The sheriff seemed startled by Spur's voice. "Why the hell not?"

"Forget it." Spur sat heavily in a rail backed chair across the room from Hughes' desk. He was tired. "Just fill me in on the ranchers' deaths."

Confused, Hughes nodded. "It was two weeks ago, Sunday morning. Can you imagine that, on the Lord's day? We don't know very much about what happened, but apparently some Navajo band —probably out hunting off Echo Creek Reservation on the richer lands to the west—stormed in on Doug MacDonald's spread—at least, they must have done that because Doug, his son Geoff, and three hands were killed before they could move to draw a weapon." Hughes shook his head. "There's something else—I've kept it quiet in town; only a few men know." He grimaced. "Those goddamned Indians weren't satisfied in just killing MacDonald. They chopped off his dick n'balls!"

Spur whistled.

"It's obvious, plain as day, that the Navajos are back to their bloodthirsty days before they were moved onto the reservation." Hughes sighed. "We found Doug lying on the ground near a stump he must've been working on, pants to his knees, all bloodied—god, there was *so much blood!* Didn't look like he had time to defend himself. I think those damned Navajos snuck up on them and killed without warning."

"Who found the bodies first? You said 'we found'."

Hughes nodded. "I happened to be headed out to the MacDonalds that day with my deputy—he's left me since. We found them a few hours after they were killed—some of the blood hadn't dried yet."

"Just the five of them—no women?" Spur asked.

"No, we found Gertrude, Doug's wife, and their eight year old daughter inside the house. Dead."

"What killed them?"

"Can't tell for sure. Most of them had arrows buried in their bodies, but some were gunshot too."

"Who examined the bodies? The local sawbones?"

Hughes shook his head. "No need. We found arrows, a bow, and moccasin prints in the sand. It was the Navajos; no doubt about it. Lots of them are using rifles now—when they can get their hands on the ammunition."

Spur frowned.

"Something the matter?" Hughes asked.

"Thinking." If most of them were killed by bullets and not arrows, it made the Indians' story more likely. "What about the Goodnights?"

"Same. Arrows and bullets, taken by surprise, all dead." He looked at Spur curiously. "Why?"

"Just working something out in my head."

Hughes shrugged. "Okay."

"I'm sure I can count on your complete cooperation and discretion," Spur said.

"Huh? Oh sure, McCoy. Of course. Anything I can do, you let me know." He drummed his fingers on the desktop.

"Good. I'm staying at the Cicily Hotel. Room Ten. My job here is secret. I don't want anyone knowing why I'm in Hanging Rocks. You got that, Hughes? Not your deputy, not your wife, nobody!"

"I'm not married," he said quickly. "Not anymore. And my deputy left me. But I understand your meaning. What I can't figure out is why you're saying it. If it's just the Navajos who killed them, why all this secrecy? There aren't any Indians in town."

Spur frowned. "Tell nobody."

The sheriff sighed. "Okay. But McCoy, hurry up and get some evidence on those Navajos so we can move the reservation hell and gone from here."

He glanced at Hughes. "Move the reservation?"

It was news to him. "Is that what the people of Hanging Rocks want?"

"You sound surprised. Of course we want it! Damnit, McCoy; get rid of the Navajo, and you get rid of our problems. They come to town at night to buy or steal whiskey, cause fights—"

Spur shook his head. "No promises, Hughes. I'll do my best. But I've got the feeling something's not right here. Don't know how."

Hughes stood. "McCoy, I wish you all the luck. And the faster you can get rid of those damned Indians the faster Grandmother Martin will be able to undress without thinking she's about to be raped." Hughes gave him a friendly smile.

As Spur moved from the office he frowned. Hughes left a bad taste in his mouth. The man wasn't suited to the job, he thought.

A commotion on the street made him look up. A black carriage raced directly toward him, a woman fumbling with the reins, waving him out of the thundering horse's path.

SIX

Spur rushed to the runaway horse pulling the terrified woman, took the reins from the woman's hands as he paced beside it, then jumped onto the buggy seat—and her lap. She squealed and moved over as he worked on the horse.

Eventually, when they'd left most of Hanging Rocks' buildings behind, the horse calmed and slowed to a trot. She snorted.

"Ohhh!" the woman exclaimed, pushing her hat down harder and smoothing out the black skirt on her knees. As she looked up at Spur her eyes were wet.

"Ma'am, are you all right?"

"Yes, yes, I'm fine," she said in a level voice. "I can't tell you how scared I was—or how thankful I am that you came along." She smiled put placed her fingertips below her swelling breasts, checking her breath.

"Just as long as you're okay," Spur said. The carriage stood still, the horse nickering but otherwise calm.

"I'm fine, really." She looked up at him suddenly. "I owe you my life!"

Spur laughed. "I don't know about that; the

horse would've run itself out eventually. The worse you might have had to do was to walk back to town."

She shrugged. "Fortunately I won't have to think about that now. I truly can't thank you enough." The woman extended her gloved hand. "I'm Margaret Bishop."

He gripped it gently. "Spur McCoy."

"I don't recognize you; have you just arrived in Hanging Rocks?"

"That's right," Spur said, jumping from the seat to look over the horse. He smoothed its mane. "Today, as a matter of fact." This seemed to be his week for meeting women who had trouble with horses, he thought wryly, and looked at her.

Margaret Bishop wasn't the prettiest woman he'd ever seen, not because her muted red hair had been blown out of careful placement by the wild ride, nor fo the color the excitement had thrown into her cheeks; but she had an indescribable aura. Her face beamed intelligence and honesty. Spur saw money and old family behind her.

Though Margaret Bishop was obviously past thirty she hadn't lost her girlish figure; Spur guessed she hadn't raised any babies.

She had green eyes and delicate features. Margaret's curved body was hidden under a black crinoline dress edged with equally black lace. As he turned his gaze to her eyes while soothing the horse he saw *her* looking at him. Spur smiled.

"She should be fine now, Mrs. Bishop." Spur patted the horse and climbed back into the carriage.

Margaret looked doubtfully at the beast. "I don't know. I may never trust that horse again. I'll have to tell Matt to bring another next time."

60

Spur smiled. "I'll be glad to drive you back to town, or until you think she's calmed."

Margaret smiled. "Really? I would appreciate it, Mr. McCoy." Her face glowed in the sun. It was flawless; not one freckle or line marred her strange beauty.

He took the reins and whip and steered the horse toward the center of town. On the way there Spur decided to do some questioning.

"Miss Bishop, I heard that two ranching families were massacred here recently. Is that true?"

Her smile faded. "Not here; it was near Hanging Rocks, though."

"How did the locals react?"

She lifted her shoulders gently. "Probably as you'd expect. They're outraged, angry, and half of them are afraid. Everyone thinks its the Navajo. The whole town is saying that, condemning them and the reservation."

"But you don't believe that?" Spur guessed.

She looked at him sharply. "It couldn't have been the Navajo, and they should know. They should know!"

Spur listened to her as he drove, not interrupting.

"The Navajo have been peaceful for years now. It's true; we haven't had much contact with them. They stay on the reservation—Echo Creek Reservation, north of here. Oh, I'll admit that there have been a few confrontations—but nothing serious."

"We treated the Navajos like dirt," Spur said. "Pushed them off their land."

"That's right!" she said. "You understand!" Margaret's mouth opened and she searched his face while he drove. "But just because we treated

61

them miserably doesn't mean that they're doing the same to us now. They didn't kill the ranching families."

"It is possible," Spur said. "Old tensions and hates die hard."

"I know that, Mr. McCoy, but not here. Not the Navajo." Margaret's voice was final.

"What makes you so sure?"

She looked to the sky. "I just am. Never mind why."

Spur had the feeling the subject was closed. "Were you headed out of town when I caught up with you?"

"Not today. I was just out riding. I do drive every week to a special place I know. It's not too far, near the stream. I feel—*safe* there.

"Aren't you afraid of Indian attacks?"

"Indian attacks? Really, Mr. McCoy!" She chuckled. "What makes you say such a thing?"

"The massacres, perhaps."

"It wasn't the Navajo who killed them; I've already told you that." Margaret sighed. "No matter what Hanging Rocks thinks, it wasn't them."

They had reached the busiest section of Broad Street. "Where to, Miss Bishop?"

"It's Mrs. Bishop," she said, smiling. "And I guess we should head back home. I wasn't going anywhere anyway." Margaret looked at the sky. "Just wanted to circle the town for a bit. It helps me think if I keep moving. Sometimes I sit in that big old house of mine and look out the windows, and—" Margaret bit her lip.

Spur steered the carriage to Oak Street according to her directions. They pulled up before an impressive single story house, built of split pine boards white washed against the grime of the high desert air.

Bordering the walk to the steps leading to the porch were twisted, stunted roses, a few splotches of color showing where buds had managed to survive long enough to bloom.

"You must come in for a cup of coffee," she said, her face radiant once again. "It's the least I can do in thanks for coming to my rescue."

"It'd be my pleasure, ma'am," Spur said. He left the carriage, held out his hand, and helped Margaret to the ground.

They walked in through an unlocked side door that led directly to to the pantry, then a huge kitchen. Margaret smiled as she pushed a wooden handle into one of the four metal plates on the stove, set it aside, filled the space below with chopped twigs and larger broken branches from a painted box beside the stove, threw in a match and set the lid in place. Margaret then filled a pot with coffee and water from the indoor pump and set it on the burner.

"This way," she said, leading him through a formal dining room into the parlor.

It was comfortably furnished, almost extravagantly so, with cherry and oak tables, chairs and bookcases; lace appropriately placed, velvet curtains pulled back and fastened with ropes to allow bright sunlight into the room. Fresh flowers stood at strategic spots in important vases.

Perhaps its most striking feature was the huge, carefully loomed Navajo rug that stretched out on the floor. It depicted clouds, mountains and a huge thunderbird, in mineral and fruit shades of yellow, orange and blue.

Spur stood by the chair indicated until Margaret

sat opposite, then sank into it.

"The coffee will be ready in a few minutes," she said, and folded her hands on her lap. "You must excuse me if I seem a bit nervous, Mr. McCoy. I don't have friends over too often. I'm a loner, I guess." Margaret gazed out the window as she spoke.

"Just relax," he said.

"I'll freely admit that when I first saw you running up to the carriage I didn't know whether you were trying to help or hurt me. Your clothing— I didn't know what to think, what kind of man you were."

Spur glanced down at his dirty jeans and sweat stained shirt. "Sorry about that, Mrs. Bishop. I just rode into town this morning and haven't had time to change."

She spread out her hands. "It's quite all right with me. I don't mind." Margaret Bishop smiled faintly. "What brings you to Hanging Rocks, Mr. McCoy?"

"I'm here on business."

She nodded slowly. "I see. Well, I certainly won't pry, if you don't wish to speak of it."

"It's private," he said.

They sat and talked of the weather for a few minutes, then Margaret smiled brightly. "Coffee's ready," she said, and rose to pour it.

An hour later, Spur opened his hotel room door, then smiled in surprise. A blonde young woman reclined on his bed, her arms nestled against each other, her torso turned to one side while her hips remained pushed firmly against the mattress.

She was naked.

As he disbelievingly closed the door behind him

64

the girl started, then stretched and half-opened her eyes.

"Frank," she said, yawning, eyelids falling again. "You're finally back."

"Who are you?"

She looked at Spur then, seemed to contemplate screaming, covered her mouth and crossed her legs while she tried to hide her ample chest with her arms.

"You're—you're not Frank," she said, wide-eyed. Her dimpled round face, showing astonishment, soon melted into more relaxed features as she looked Spur over.

"No. This is Room Ten, isn't it?"

"Yes. But you're not Frank Cousins!"

She squirmed on the bed, and as she moved her clenched knee from side to side Spur saw occasional flashes of her hair patch. A nipple poked through her fingers.

"Who is this Frank Cousins?" Spur asked, enjoying the show.

She lifted one shoulder, then slid back on the bed and pushed up to lean against the headboard, still half trying to cover her naked body. "Well, he's a—a friend." She sighed. "Oh, what the hell. He's a *good* friend. Do you know what I mean?"

"Yeah," Spur said, still looking her over. "I guess Frank checked out last night," he said, remembering the manager's comment.

"I guess so." She pouted. "Frank was staying here all last week. He didn't say he was leaving town." She looked at him guardedly. "He told the manager he'd lost his key, so he got another one, and gave me his." The woman indicated the table to the left of the bed. A skeleton key lay there. "But I haven't been able to find Frank for a few days. I took the chance he was still here." Her gaze lowered from his head and rested on his midsection, then moved further down.

Spur grunted. Even though she was young, probably eighteen, she knew her way around men. Why not? "Like what you see?" he asked in his deepest voice. It was startling to be ogled by a young woman.

She laughed and looked up at him. "Boy, you sure don't mince words, do you? But yes. Yes, I like you."

"How old are you?"

She pouted. "You men always ask my age," she said. "What does it matter if I'm 21, or 16? But I'm eighteen, and I know how to have a good time."

"I'm glad." He moved closer to the bed, slowly, as she stared up at him. "What your name?"

"Caroline."

He had reached the edge of the bed. "Well, Caroline, since your friend Frank didn't show up, how about me? Would you like to have a good time with me?"

She hesitated for a moment, then threw her arms out to both sides and spread her legs. "Oh yes! I thought you'd never ask!"

Spur fell onto the bed on top of her, sending Caroline giggling as she removed his hat, sat it on the table, and then fumbled with his shirt buttons.

He drove his groin against hers, rough jeans on soft skin, the contact hardening him to full erection. Caroline turned her head as Spur bit down the side of her neck. She pushed her tongue into her ear and sucked it while Spur moaned in combined surprise and pleasure.

Their mouths almost met, but Caroline put her

hand between them. Spur pulled back.

"What the hell?" he asked.

"I never kiss a man until I know his name."

"Spur McCoy," he said, and dropped back onto her.

Their lips fused as he slid his tongue between them into her warm mouth.

Caroline finally succeeded in unbuttoning his shirt, and pushed it off while Spur obediently held his arms back. She then reached down to his fly, played with his buckle, unfastened it and then pushed his groin off hers three inches. She pulled the cloth away from the steel buttons and eagerly shoved down his jeans and short underdrawers.

"Mr. McCoy, what a big present you have for me!" Caroline said in awe as she stared at his erection.

"It's all yours," Spur said huskily, his throat suffused with desire. "You unwrapped it." He kicked the pants from his legs and then pressed down onto her, sighing as her firm young body welcomed his.

The moment their skin made contact, his firm penis jabbing against her thigh and belly, Caroline shivered. She seemed to have difficulty keeping her eyes fully opened as Spur stared at her breasts, then stroked one, squeezing the nipple gently.

Spur put his mouth over one breast, sucked hard, and chewed on the now firm tip while fondling its twin. He switched several times, continually grinding away against her, as she moaned and ran her hands over his powerful body.

Caroline wiggled below him, trying to position herself so his penis would thrust up inside her. After a few moments of failure while he continued to feast on her breasts, she slapped his back.

"Goddamn, Spur, that feels great, but you're teasing me!" she said in a high, excited voice. "Frank never teased me this way. Hell, I want you to put that big thing of yours into me! You're driving me crazy!" She pulled his warm mouth from her breasts and kissed him, then gently bit his chin and ran her teeth against his stubbly jaw. "Please fuck me, Spur!" The words hissed against his ear.

Spur reached down, grabbed himself at its base, and plunged inside her splayed legs.

"Hot damn!" Caroline said as he entered her. "Yes, that's the feeling, that's the feeling. Oh yes!" She seemed to explode. "That's it! Fuck me silly, Spur! Ride me!" Her breaths were counterpointed with shivers. Caroline's delicate hands gripped Spur's waist and pulled him toward her, trying to bury him even deeper inside.

"Anything you want, Caroline," McCoy said, wondering if his neighbor in Room Eight was listening. Hell, he didn't care.

He stroked with vigor, riding high, rubbing against her clitoris until Caroline's nails snaked down his back and her mouth hung open, body tense, eyes tightly shut. She relaxed a second later, then a storm of passion swept through her as Spur touched her in the right places.

"Don't stop!" she managed to choke out, grabbing his hips and holding on.

Spur had to look away from her attractive, youthful face, knowing he'd be done sooner than he wanted if he didn't. He slowed his pace, sending up a squeal from Caroline almost immediately.

"Harder and faster!" she said, her face flushed. "Spur, I want to feel your dick in my throat. Shove

68

it all the way in until I can taste it! Don't disappoint me!"

He could tell she was challenging him, pretending to be teasing. Spur knew he could rise to it. In answer, he moved his arms down between her ankles, pushed them out and slowly slid her legs up until her knees bent and her ankles lay against his shoulders. On his toes and hands Spur jabbed into her in short, deep strokes, alternating with longer, savage pounding that made Caroline gasp.

Her body skidded along the sheets as he rammed into her, sweat flying off his hair. Caroline groaned and shook her head, clenching his biceps, riding with him as her body screamed with pleasure and she shook through another orgasm.

His hairy belly slapped against Caroline's stomach for the hundredth time as she lifted her head and licked his chin and neck, lapping up the sweat there. Spur's body shook and he grunted away for ten seconds while shooting his load into the young woman's body.

Moving his arms to his sides after his earth shattering moment, Spur let Caroline's lower body slip to the bed. He pushed his open lips against hers and they exchanged moist breath for a few seconds before he licked her lips, then pressed his slick cheek against hers.

As he spasmed inside her again she groaned and bit his earlobe. Their bodies seemed to join, sweating together, as Spur held the girl and waited for his heart to slow.

He pulled wetly from her. Caroline looked at him with sex-diffused eyes as he lay on his side next to her.

"Did you have a good time?" Spur asked.

"Oh yes." Caroline laid a hand on his chest, then shook her head. "What am I doing? I should be going home." She started to rise.

Spur grabbed her hand. "You sure? I thought maybe we could go again."

Caroline laughed. "I wish I had the time," she said, "but my father will miss me if I'm not back home in ten minutes." She rose, then kissed his shrinking penis, and walked to the chair onto which she'd earlier draped her clothing.

After quickly dressing, with a few comments to Spur, she turned to the door. "Be seeing you, Spur. I promise."

"When?" he asked, rising and walking naked to the door.

"Soon." She kissed him again, screwed up her face and left.

Caroline, Spur said to himself. Her name was Caroline. Caroline *who?*

SEVEN

Chief Eagle Feather's hogan sat two hundred yards south of the main cluster of shelters on the Echo Creek Reservation. Ten miles from Hanging Rocks, the reservation consisted of five hundred thousand acres of rolling land broken up by shattered mountains, and was choicer than that of many Indian relocation centers: there were plentiful cedar and juniper, year long streams, even wildlife: deer, antelope, big-horned sheep and others. Unlike the more agricultural Apaches, the Navajos had always been strict hunters. They'd rather hunt an animal down than pull a potato from the ground.

The chief squatted inside his round shelter, his wrinkled chin resting on his knees before the fire in the center of the packed earth floor. No matter how warm the air became during the day his bones ached with cold. Two blankets and a poncho couldn't cut the chill, for it came from within. When Chief Eagle Feather noticed that while he froze some of the braves in his tribe went naked to the waist about their daily tasks, he had a revelation.

He was growing old.

The chief sighed and looked up to the circle of blue sky that shone through the central hole in the hogan's dirt and log roof. After all these years old age shouldn't come as a surprise to him, but it had. He'd lost count of the moon cycles; at some point he remembered the experience of being young, but that was long ago and the images and feelings were misty.

Eagle Feather continued to look up as he heard a brave enter his hogan.

"Eagle Feather!" the voice demanded.

He didn't need to glance at the brash newcomer. "Rainbow Dream."

"Look at me, old man!" he said. When the chief didn't comply, he roared. "Then I will say it to your back. I have decided. We will raid the round eyes."

Eagle Feather looked at Rainbow Dream coolly, staring at the tall, stocky Indian's triumphant expression.

When Eagle Feather didn't respond to his statement, Rainbow Dream moved to face the man. "Have your ears left you, along with your mind?"

The eyes that flashed up to look onto his face weren't those of an elder; they drew Rainbow Dream in. Sparks of light reflecting on them from the fire seemed to make Eagle Feather's pupils pulse and dilate.

Rainbow Dream stared at the chief's face and

saw his features change slightly; his nose lengthened into a cruel yellow beak, the eyes narrowed to gleaming black orbs, feathers pushing out through the man's pores.

Rainbow Dream shook his head, blinking. The vision vanished.

"Do you use sorcerer's tricks on me now, Eagle Feather?" he asked lightly, laughing off the incident with a tight throat.

"They are not tricks," the chief said. "You know that." He lowered his gaze to the fire and contemplated it through wrinkle enshrouded eyes.

The Indian seemed angered by the old man's lack of response. "Listen to me, old coyote!" Rainbow Dream shouted. "I don't care what you say. We're raiding the white man's town at light. You don't have to ride with us if you're scared of their magic."

He looked up sharply. "It's not their magic." Eagle Feather's shoulders slumped as he felt his vitality wane. "You are not chief yet, Rainbow Dream."

"It won't be long now," he said. "Soon you'll have to journey to the mountains. Why not today, old man?" Rainbow Dream stared at Eagle Feather, his ugly, scarred face twisted with cruel pleasure. "You're old and don't know what you're saying."

"The tribe will never follow you."

The brave laughed. "We will see. I *know* they will! We're tired of peace; if this is the only life we have left, we'd rather ride the way of war again." He paused. "What do you fear?"

The chief stared hard at Rainbow Dream. If the Navajo gave the whites the slightest reason their army would come and all would be ended. Rainbow Dream was hurrying that along.

He broke his gaze. "You," he said. The chief sighed. "You will finish the *Dine*, the Navajo. The round eyes will descend like snow and crush us."

"No! We were born to this land! Our ancestors hunted and lived and coupled and died on the land! These pale men can't take our land away from us, or from the Gods! We will take back what is right-fully ours—tear down the buildings, tend our orchards!"

"It is done. All is passed. Nothing can change now. Leave the round eyes in peace and they will do the same to us."

Rainbow Dream shook his head erratically, send-ing his long black hair rustling. "No, stupid old coyote! We will still their heart. We will go to their camp and stab them while they sleep."

"And then the army will come," the chief said sadly. "And they will stamp us into the dirt. A million men, the blue clothed man said. That has to be more people than we have." Chief Eagle Feather frowned, pulling some of his facial wrinkles taut.

The younger man slapped his chest, then his head. "Sunstruck. Our chief is sunstruck. You stay in here where you won't fall down on the trail. *We go*. It is said. At first light." With a firm glance he left the hogan, his back flap flying.

Chief Eagle Feather looked at the blue again, and prayed to the Gods of the mountains, sky, lightning and fire, that he would find the courage to kill Rainbow Dream that night.

Spur's belly pushed tighter against his belt as he left the table after his two-bit noon meal. The beef, onion and carrot stew, mashed potatoes and two helpings of peach shortcake had more than satisfied his craving for food. He had been walking down the street, smelled stew bubbling inside a boarding house's kitchen, and followed it in. He joined ten other men at a long, plain table and soon dug in.

He was surprised by the peaches; they were fresh, not canned.

"Where'd you come by the peaches?" he asked the mistress of the boarding house on his way out.

The plump woman smiled. "Delicious, aren't they? They come from the peach orchards just outside of town. You know, the ones the injuns planted way back when? They just loved those peaches, I hear. Of course, now *we've* got them. It's only right."

Spur looked at her peculiarly. "How's that?"

The stout woman smiled and cocked her head. "You know, like everyone else knows. *They're not really human.*" She winked, patted his shoulder, and moved to the sink.

The peaches flipped in his stomach as Spur continued out the kitchen door as he imagined the woman gunning down Navajo in her spare time. Stepping into the bright alley Spur turned right toward the street. As he approached it he heard a loud voice complaining about the Indians.

Spur slowed his pace, leaned against the freshly

painted wall, dug his hands into his pockets, and stared at the sky. Listening.

"Christ, Fairfax! You really think so?" a rather high man's voice said.

"Hell yes! It's obvious to me and to anybody that thinks about it that they're dangerous, just like rattlensnakes. What do you do when you see a rattlesnake?"

"Kill it," the man said slowly.

"You're goddamned right you do!" Fairfax said in a booming voice. "Might as well do the same thing to those goddamned savages, right?"

"Maybe."

"Maybe! Maybe? God*damn! God*damn! Those redmen are out there on the reservation, plotting to rape every woman in town, burn down the buildings and kill all the men! How'd you like to see some red skinned man between your daughter's legs?"

"Shut your fucking mouth, Fairfax!" the man said testily.

"See? You wouldn't stand for it."

"You're goddamned right I wouldn't!"

"Hell, just thinking about it's got you all fired up," Fairfax continued in a smoother voice. "Right? So let's make sure it never happens."

"I don't know. We've got them outnumbered. And hell, with Fort Prescott nearby I don't see how we're in any real danger."

"Forget it, then," Fairfax said. "If you can't see the danger, hell; just forget it."

There was a pause.

"Then why did you bring it up in the first place?"

"It was on my mind, since Doug MacDonald and his family were killed by the Navajos. I didn't know old Goodnight, but Doug seemed like a good man. We drank a few in the Placer one hot afternoon.''

"Hell, every afternoon's hot around here," the man's friend said.

Spur decided the conversation was winding down. He pushed away from the building and walked into the street, paused as if trying to find his way, and saw the two men sitting on the edge of the boardwalk to his left. He moved in that direction.

As he passed the men spoke again.

"Hell, Fairfax," the one began, and turned to look at Spur as he walked by. Fairfax followed suit.

Spur returned the glance but kept moving. He burned Fairfax's face into his memory: the hard, unshaven jaw, line rimmed eyes, heavy brows and thin, gray flecked moustache that covered his upper lip. Fairfax's face was grim as Spur passed.

He took a turn at the next corner, thinking over the man's words. Fairfax was definitely an Indian hater. It also seemed he was trying to spread such sentiments in Hanging Rocks. Why? What could the man possibly gain?

Maybe he really was afraid of the imagined threat and wanted the Indians out of there for safety's sake.

But he could also be the one who'd killed the Navajo or, perhaps, the ranchers.

Then again, the man had nothing to lose. Few whites openly liked the Navajo; the two races were isolated from each other save for occasional contact. If there was a movement to have the reservation relocated it would certainly be by trying to drum up supporters.

But Fairfax was talking about killing the

Indians, not moving them. He certainly didn't seem to be secretive about his views. Alcohol may have increased the volume of his voice, but not the feelings behind it.

Spur walked down another block, greeting several pairs of women and young couples arm in arm strolling. He ducked into Sheriff Hughes' office. The man looked up at him in surprise.

"McCoy, good to see you."

"Same here. What do you think about a man named Fairfax?"

Hughes looked at him in surprise. "What do you mean?"

Spur slid into a chair. "What kind of man is he? Does he kick dogs and hate babies?"

The sheriff sunk into his chair. "He's a good man. Drinks, but then everyone does. He's bedded a few other men's wives, but his own wife Shirley has been screwing the bald bartender at the Longbar for the past three months." Hughes shrugged. "I don't suppose he's better or worse than the rest of the men in Hanging Rocks. Why?"

"Nothing. I overheard a conversation in the street and his name came up."

Hughes frowned and stood. "What've you found out so far—about the MacDonalds and the Goodnights?"

"Some. I'm heading out to the ranches today, so I need directions."

"No problem," Hughes said. "Ride east until Broad Street peters out into a trail. About three miles out you'll come to a track heading north. Follow it until you find a barbed wire fence. Ride beside it for a mile and you'll see the buildings of the MacDonald spread. About two miles due north you'll find the Goodnight place."

"Thanks," Spur said, memorizing the directions. "Hey, you gonna tell me why you're asking about Leon Fairfax or not?" Hughes asked.

Spur smiled and left.

McCoy found the fence and rode next to it. In a few minutes he saw a huge red barn dominating the bottom of the valley, with jagged red cliffs rising on all sides. A silvery river cut across the area, running within one hundred feet of the farmhouse, a massive two story structure. A large bunkhouse, smokehouse, several corrals, pens and other outbuildings were scattered around the area, and miles of cattle proof fence sharply defined the ranch's limitations.

All seemed peaceful at the ranch—the windmill shook and rotated, slapping wood against wood ceaselessly as Spur rode up to the buildings. Closer, he could see the destruction—the windows shot out in the farmhouse, the front door torn off its hinges, blood staining the ground outside, deeper reddish brown patches on the light brown soil.

Spur dismounted, tied the stallion to a rail, and walked to the house. The front door lay on the ground, the entrance seemingly a wound. He walked inside and felt, rather than knew that the house was *dead*. No one lived there.

Dust swirled up as a breeze blew in through the shattered windows; in just two weeks nearly everything in the house had been covered with dust. Though some furniture and other articles had obviously been removed, the house seemed fairly intact. Spur found nothing in it to help him.

He moved from what he took to be the master bedroom and went outside. McCoy stopped when he saw a flash of white nestled in the dirt. He stooped and lifted it. As the earth fell away a pattern emerged; it was an inch-wide, half-foot long piece of beadwork, and the design was unmistakeably Navajo.

Spur grimaced and put the piece in his pocket, then made a close inspection of the ground. He saw a few arrowheads, some broken arrows, a bow. Though wind had obliterated the prints in most of the area, in some small protected spots Spur clearly saw moccasin prints.

But as he looked closer at a near perfect impression in the dirt, Spur sensed that something was wrong with it. The heel area seemed heavier, deeper, than the Navajo prints he'd seen before.

That was it. Spur nodded. The men who wore these moccasin had placed most of their weight on their heels, not the balls of their feet.

As far as he could tell, Navajos hadn't worn those moccasins. Maybe the story he'd heard from the Indians on his way to Hanging Rocks wasn't so unbelievable after all.

Someone had murdered the MacDonalds and, as he was sure he'd find when he rode there that someone had made it seem to be the work of the Navajo. Who?

Leon Fairfax?

Spur walked to the wall of the house and was struck by the number of bullets he found embedded in the wood or that had found a soft spot and had plowed through.

It seemed the Indians hadn't used bows and arrows to kill the ranchers.

Spur rode quickly to the Goodnight ranch and found the same signs there. Someone had done the minimum, as if he thought that if he wore

80

moccasins and threw around a few Navajo artifacts that the whites would believe that the Indians had massacred them.

It could have been Fairfax, especially if he was behind some effort to push the reservation from Hanging Rocks. Spur didn't know if he believed the man's talk about killing the Navajos like rattlesnakes, but he didn't doubt Fairfax's hatred of the people.

EIGHT

Stanton approached the ten pew church with disgust. Just before entering the small, stark, white washed building he spat. The saliva sizzled on the hot sand.

Stanton found him at the organ, dusting the yellowed ivory keys.

Reverend Edward Yasger looked up from his work. His face cooled considerably from his normal welcoming expression as he watched Stanton approach him.

"Come to pray, Mr. Stanton?" he asked, then turned back to the keyboard.

Stanton grabbed Yasger's shoulders and violently twisted him around, released him and chuckled. "Hell no, Yasger! Just stopped in to make sure you remember what I told you the other night."

Yasger's face was blank. "What was that?"

Stanton exploded. "You know what the hell I'm talking about! When you came to me and said you was going to start preaching that Indians have souls, that they're human beings!" Stanton punched the minister lightly in the stomach. "And I told you you weren't going to do that. I'm here to make sure you keep that idea to yourself, this and every other Sunday, when you're in here spouting your bullshit!"

Yasger's face showed pain. "Please, Mr. Stanton!" Yasger said. "This is the house of hte Lord!"

Stanton snorted. "House of the Lord! Hell, I own this place. It's *my* house." He paused and stuck his fists on his waist. "You know, I guess I had you figured wrong. I swear when you showed in town and came to me for a loan to build your church, you weren't no more a Christian than I was. Hell, it was obvious you were running from something or someone—just pretending to be a preacher. Now you seem to believe in all this."

Yasger smiled. "That's right, Mr. Stanton, if you have to know the truth. I've been washed in the blood of Jesus Christ. I'm still a sinner, but my soul is safe." He shook his head. "I'm surprised you didn't notice earlier."

"What the fuck happened to you, Yasger?" Stanton asked, scratching his groin. "You used to be a regular man. Now you're starting to believe all this shit—" He waved his hand at the altar, "—and I don't like the change."

Yasger leaned against the organ and folded his arms. "Mr. Stanton, it's out of your hands. There's nothing you can do about it."

The man smiled wickedly. "You don't seem like the man who came into town three years ago, running. I remember later hearing that a Methodist minister alone on the trail was killed and stripped bareass naked of his clothing, even his Bible. That must have happened a day or so before you arrived in Hanging Rocks." Stanton's smile changed to a grimace. "I always figured you

84

killed that minister to get his clothes, so no one would suspect you. What were you running from, Yasger, three years ago?''

The man stiffened and backed away from Stanton. He glanced at the altar behind him. ''That was a long time ago,'' he said. ''The Lord has cleansed me of my sins.''

Stanton studied the man. He was saying the words, but Yasger didn't quite seem to believe them. ''What was this *sin* of yours?''

Yasger hesitated.

''Hell, I thought telling things like that was good for the soul, to get it off your chest. Come on, Yasger. What'd you do? What made you clear the hell out of wherever you were and run to Hanging Rocks, killing a preacher on the way?''

The minister turned his head and sighed, then clasped his hands before him waist level and walked to the altar. A plain silver cross and candlesticks sat on the wooden table, the latter's flickering flames enlivening its starkness.

''Stanton, I can't.'' The man looked away

''Yasger, you want me to run you out of town? You know I can. Hell, I'lll make up some sort of story about how you like to watch the boys at the swimming hole—I'll make it disgusting. Then you'll be running again, Yasger.'' He grabbed the man's shoulder. ''Tell me!''

He wrenched from the contact and spun. ''Okay. I might as well. You know everything else.'' He swallowed. ''I was in Tucson, had a job as a bartender. The boss' wife was the most beautiful woman I'd ever seen, and I lusted after her. For months I watched her come and go, never letting my hunger show. Then, one night I couldn't take it anymore. I finished work and went to her house.

The boss was still at the saloon so I knew she'd be alone. I didn't try to hide my intentions—she could see my, my arousal as I stood at the door.

"Still, she invited me in and we sat in her parlor. After a few minutes I couldn't stand it anymore. I fell on top of her and struggled to rip her clothing off.

"At first she laughed, telling me I shouldn't drink on the job and that I should sleep it off. Then she screamed as I felt—" Yasger's head lowered. "She screamed as I felt between her legs. I didn't know what I was doing; she was yelling and struggling so I punched her once to make her shut up. She fell back, hit her head on the couch's arm. She was out, so I pulled off her clothes and raped her.

"Only after I'd finished—did I realize she was—was dead." Yasger choked. "I'd—I'd killed my boss' wife, then raped her!" he said hoarsely.

Stanton whistled as Yasger ended his speech. He couldn't believe it. After a moment he slapped Yasger's arm and roared.

"Shit, Yasger, that's some story! Wait until I tell Colby!"

The minister looked at Stanton for a moment, shocked, then turned and knelt before the altar. He folded his hands and bowed his head.

Stanton's chuckles subsided. "Remember, Yasger, no preaching about the Indians. If you spill one word everyone in town'll know what you did in Tucson. You know I'll tell them, too."

Yasger's lips moved in silent prayer. He made no response.

Stanton savagely kicked the man's buttocks. Yasger jolted forward, his arms landing on the altar. His stomach crashed into the table's edge, and his breath blew out a candle as Stanton strode out of the stuffy, dismal church.

Goddamn Christian! Stanton thought, and spat.

He walked home, enjoying the fresh air and the busy streets. Buggies rattled along, horses frisked outside the Longbar and Placer saloons, and there was a brisk trade at the stores and bank.

He walked into his home at Second and Oak streets. Caroline, a stunning young blonde of eighteen, looked up from her knitting and smiled half-heartedly.

"Hello, Caroline," he said with his usual brusque tone.

"Hi, father." The young woman's voice was sullen.

He strode past her into his office, shut the door, poured two shots of whiskey and drank half the glass.

Someone knocked at his door.

"Come in," he said.

Caroline walked in and looked at her father stubbornly. "I want to ask you a question," she said, her face a study in tension.

"Go ahead," Stanton sipped his whiskey and eyed her curiously.

"What are you doing?" Caroline clutched the yarn and a six-inch nearly complete square before her.

"What are you talking about?" he asked lightly.

"Why are people coming over late at night? Why do I have to stay upstairs after ten o'clock and not come down until morning? And why are you always shouting at something or someone?" Her cheeks reddened as she spoke.

Stanton, startled by her appearance and questions, set his glass on the bar.

"You never used to shout," she said. "You were always kind and good. Now you're—you're mean." She shook her head. "I don't know what I'm saying. I'm doing this all wrong."

He smiled and went to her, then stroked her pale ringlets. "Caroline, I'm busy with a project right now. A big project."

"Another building?" she asked.

"No."

"Is it important?"

Stanton's voice was firm. "Yes. I wouldn't waste my time on it if it wasn't."

"But what—"

He clenched her shoulders. "Trust your father," he looked at her intently.

Caroline finally turned from his gaze. "Okay. I guess I don't have a choice."

"That's a good girl." He released her and retrieved his drink. As he drained the drink he watched Caroline walk to the door, pause and glance back.

"You look tired," Stanton said.

She smiled faintly. "I can't sleep at night."

"Too restless?"

She shook her head. "No, it's—" Caroline didn't finish the sentence. "Never mind. I'll be fine." She left.

Stanton scratched the back of his neck under the stiff shirt collar and frowned. The Navajos were ready to attack and his daughter was having problems sleeping. Not surprising. She must know the danger she's in—that they all faced as long as Echo Creek lay only ten miles away.

Those savages were keeping his daughter from sleeping, he thought, but not for long. Soon Caroline and every other woman and child could rest easily—after his army had either wiped out or driven back all the Navajos, and the whole area was safe and free of the taint of Indians.

Despite some problems, like Yasger's new ideas and the incident with Frank Cousins and Buck at the meeting, his plans were running well. Soon he'd have an organized unit of men, then another and another, and together they'd stack up Indian bodies.

Stanton's face flushed at the thought, and he felt an unusual sensation: he was growing stiff. That didn't happen too often lately, but Stanton didn't try to understand why he was aroused. He slapped the glass down on the bar, strode out of his house with a word to Caroline, and went to the Longbar Saloon.

Judith sat downing a ginger ale near the piano. The bar wasn't busy, since it was early in the day. Stanton pointed to the woman, who slowly rose and smiled at him. She wasn't pretty, with sagging breasts, fleshy neck and sallow skin, but she was better than pulling it off himself in the outhouse.

She climbed the stairs and he followed her. In a moment they were in her room. He roughly shut the curtains, then turned to look at her.

Judith had already begun shrugging off her dress and was soon naked. She walked to a small closet and removed a fringed leather dress, ornamented with beadwork, then smiled knowingly as she slipped it on, pulled the combs from her black hair and let it flow around her shoulders.

"What do you want, Stanton?" she asked.

"Shut up and lay down!" he barked, fumbling with his clothing. He released his imprisoned penis and flopped down on top of the woman.

As Stanton took her roughly, pounding without

89

mercy into her, he didn't think who she really was.
She was a nameless Navajo woman, submitting to
his superiority, and he almost smelled the Indian
campfires as he raped the defenseless heathen.

NINE

Dave Colby sat slumped in a chair in his room at the Stanton mansion. Situated on the top floor facing south it was miserably hot nearly year round. Colby hadn't brought anything with him when he had come to live with the Stantons, and his room reflected that—painted a dull brown, the walls were bare and the shining wood floor was empty save for the tiny bed, basin stand and the uncomfortable, straight backed chair in which Colby sat.

Stop it, he thought, staring hard at his partial erection. He closed his eyes in sexual torment, only to again see Caroline Stanton bending over to hand him a cup of coffee at breakfast that morning. Her white dress had fallen three inches down her front, giving him a short but breathtaking view of her pink nipples. She was smiling sweetly as he looked up to her eyes seconds later, then she turned away from him and was gone before he could react.

He tingled at the memory of the other times Caroline had seemed to tease him, to invite him to ravage her. Colby leaned his head back and tried to relax.

Caroline had often glanced at his crotch—he was

91

sure of it. At first it seemed accidental, and she never commented about it. Neither had he, out of possible embarrassment—she was Stanton's eighteen year old daughter, after all.

Colby thought of the night when he'd shucked his clothes and stood in the tin pail in his room, stark naked, pouring kettle warmed water over his body, splashing off the stinging lye soap suds. It was the first bath he'd had in a week and was glad of it.

He had been shaking his head, spreading water through the room, when the door opened and Caroline walked in. She had stared at his crotch as he stood frozen for several seconds, watching water drip from his penis.

As Caroline gazed at him Colby had felt himself stiffening but was unable to stop the process. Caroline laughed, mumbled an apology, and made a quick escape.

He hadn't left his room for hours that night. For weeks afterward Colby wondered if she'd laughed out of disappointment or to cover her shyness. Hell, he just couldn't figure out women.

Now, this morning, she had shown that other side of her—the fancy, wild woman locked within a young girl's body. Colby rose, his erection stabbing painfully against the rough cut of his trousers as he walked to the window where he kept a bottle of whiskey. The liquor glowed amber in the morning sun beside a streaked glass.

He poured a shot and replaced the bottle, then returned to his chair. Colby drank, hoping the whiskey would make him forget about trying to bed Caroline. If she wasn't completely willing he'd lose everything, and that bothered him.

It wasn't only the fact that Stanton paid him

twenty dollars a month plus room and board and all the whiskey he could drink, though he'd been considerably poorer.

No. It was because, as much as he hated to admit it, certainly to the man himself, Colby looked up to Stanton as a shining example of how anyone could go from poverty to wealth. Through his limitless capacity to concentrate on one project at a time he had dug his fortune and built up this city. The man wouldn't have to work another day in his life, Colby thought, not unenvious.

Dave Colby's own background was easy to sum: the son of poor dairy farmers in upstate New York, at twenty-one he left his father's business, told the woman he'd promised to marry three years previously to *fuck herself*, and left for Arizona where he thought he'd make it rich—one way or another. New York state bored him, farming bored him and his family was driving him out of his skull.

He never regretted leaving them behind, and had managed to shift for himself until two years ago, when he met Stanton, started drinking with the man regularly and finally came under his employ.

Stanton had described his official job as maintenance man and caretaker. In other words, when something went wrong in the house, Colby was expected to take care of it. He'd nailed down some shingles, rehung a door and painted the house once. That summed up his maintenance work to date.

So he skated by, living well, doing nothing but drinking and whoring with the tired women in the local saloons. He never felt guilty about living off Stanton—if the man was willing to pay him a fortune he wasn't going to argue.

But for the last year Stanton had admitted he

had other plans in mind for Colby—something he wouldn't talk about. Now he thought it might have something to do with his army—and his aim to wipe out the Navajos. That suited him must fine.

One of the reasons that Colby had left New York state was because nothing happened there. One day ran into the next with unwavering regularity, and he had felt stifled by his life and surroundings. An Indian war should perk him up. Colby sipped whiskey and tried to forget the pounding between his legs as he returned to the present.

Colby suddenly realized his bedroom was hot, stifling. He rose unsteadily and walked to the window, set the empty glass beside the bottle, slid the window open and sighed as a gentle breeze swirled in, cooling his slick face.

With it came a woman's voice—sighing, then laughing. Caroline. What was she up to?

Her bedroom lay directly beside his; she must have her window open too.

As her voice ran through him Colby felt his knees shake. He poured another shot, gulped it down, slammed the glass on the windowsill and stormed out of his room. He walked ten feet to her door and stopped before it.

Colby lifted his hand to knock, then hesitated. He couldn't hear her voice. Had it been Caroline? What was she doing anyway?

Maybe he shouldn't disturb her. He'd open the door just a crack to see what she was up to.

Colby dropped to his knees before the door and held the knob with both hands, then slowly twisted it to the right. The door opened noiselessly. He swung it inward and saw Caroline lying on her bed, dressed in a camisole, under which he saw her firm nipples and, lower, between her spread legs, the crotch of her bloomers.

He nearly groaned as he saw her hand slide across her mound, her fingernails scratching the satin and the sensitive areas below.

Christ, Colby thought. Was she just scratching, or was she feeling herself?

She moaned and removed her hand, then stretched. Must be asleep, Colby thought. Then she stood, looked directly at him, and walked to the door.

Run, Colby thought. She's going to scream and get the old man up here. But he didn't move. Caroline might be the boss's daughter, but he had to know today, right now, if she was going to give it to him.

As he stood, tense, while she slowly approached him, swinging her hips, Colby wondered whether she'd slam the door in his face or open it wider.

Caroline reached the door, stared at him for a moment, then lifted her arm and laid her wrist on the top of her head. She tilted her chin upward and looked at him with softly smouldering eyes.

"Hello, Dave."

He smiled nervously. "Hi, Caroline."

"Sure is hot today," she said.

"Yeah, it is. I opened my window and heard you laughing."

She smiled. "I was remembering something while I was undressing. It's too hot to wear clothes. Don't you think?"

"Sure."

"That doesn't shock you, does it, David?"

He shook his head. "No! Not really. I mean, not at all." He couldn't help but stare at her breasts under the thin chemise. "I hope you don't mind my looking."

"Of course not," she said. "Men should look at

95

women. That's healthy and natural." Caroline continued to stare at him unblinkingly. "In fact, why don't you come in and get out of those clothes? You might as well strip down to your underwear. Fair enough?"

Colby nodded. To hell with what Stanton would think if he found them together. The old man said he'd be locked in his office all day with business.

He moved into her room, closed the door behind him, and pulled off his shirt and boots, then his pants, and stood uncertainly before her.

Caroline glanced at he obvious bulge in the pouch of his short underdrawers. She smiled. "It looks like you're hot too. Boiling hot." Her lips pursed, and she seemed to blow a kiss to his crotch.

Colby reached for her then, but she backed out of his arms. He cursed.

"Teasing me again, are you, Caroline?"

"What are you talking about?" Her voice was innocent.

"You know." He stared at her thinly covered breasts.

"I don't know what you're saying." Her eyes were wide, lips pursed. "I just asked if you wanted to get cool."

"Look, Caroline, you're confusing me," Colby said, feeling his impending erection shrink.

She laughed.

"Does your father know how you dress—or I should say *un*dress—when he's busy with work?"

"No. I don't always do this, anyway. I mean, you've seen me with my clothes on around here."

"Yeah, and you've seen me naked. Remember that time when you—"

She nodded. "I remember every inch." Her little girl act was gone.

"Really?" Colby asked. He felt it pulse, stir.

"Yes."

"So?" he said, reaching for her breasts.

"I—I can't." Her siren's eyes faded. Caroline was again an eighteen year old girl under her father's thumb.

"Why the hell not? You certainly want to. You can't deny that. Christ, you've been staring at my prick for months now." Colby knew he could talk her into it if he tried hard enough. She was more than willing.

"Do you know what my father would do if he found out?"

"We can keep a secret," Colby said.

"No. I wouldn't be able to look at you at dinner without thinking of—"

"Does your father know you're not a virgin?" Colby asked bluntly, his eyes cold. Damn her for teasing me!

"What makes you think I'm not a virgin?" Caroline asked, anger streaking her face.

"Cut the crap, Caroline." Colby felt the whiskey. "It's obvious you know what you're doing. You're not just pretending, or teasing me. How many men have you slept with? And how are you making sure you don't get pregnant?"

"That's none of your damned business, David Colby!" Caroline pushed her shoulders back, unintentionally highlighting her breasts. "Sure, I'd love to get that long thing of yours into me. I'll admit it! But you know what my father would do!"

Colby shook his head. "So why have you been practically begging me for it for the last few months? Why have you been torturing me, showing me your breasts, staring between my legs?"

"I—well, I mean, I—I can't help myself!" Caroline blushed. "Oh, I don't mean you're any Greek god or anything. I've seen handsomer men."

"Thanks a lot!"

"But it's something about you—I don't know what it is. Maybe it's just because you're close by, forbidden." She shook her head. "Maybe it's something in your eyes."

"Or between my legs," Colby said. To hell with what she wanted! He'd make her beg for it. He reached down and swiftly unbuttoned his underdrawers, releasing his erection as they fell to the floor.

As it swung up Caroline gasped. "Oh, Dave!" she said, took one step backward, a silly grin on her face, then moved toward him.

The door suddenly opened. "Caroline!"

They watched Michael Stanton walk into the room. Colby blanched and hastily stuffed himself back into his shorts. Caroline looked at her father bemusedly.

"Well?" Stanton asked in a stern voice.

After a silence of ten seconds while Colby fumbled with buttons and stiff cotton cloth, Caroline spoke.

"Rape," she said, yawning.

"Jesus Christ, it's a goddamn injun!"

Spur heard the shout as he passed an alley and looked down it. Near its end, two young white men had cornered an old Navajo man who was wrapped in a blanket, standing against a brick wall. The men taunted him.

"I guess we oughta kill him," a fair haired skinny man with a blotch covered face said to his

98

stocky companion, who constantly squinted to bring the aged Indian into focus.

"Sure, I guess we should," he said with enthusiasm. He drew his six-shooter and held it uncertainly before him, looking at his companion.

The taller of the two approached the Navajo and waved his Colt in the man's face. "Well, Injun? You gonna tell us why you're here? What are you doing in Hanging Rocks? They kick you off the reservation? You gonna rape our women?"

The fat one laughed as the Indian stared blankly at them, clutching the blanket to him.

Spur walked down the alley towards them.

"Come on, you lost your tongue or something?"

"Ah hell; just kill him and let's get a drink," the shorter man said. "I don't think he understands a damn word we say."

"The hell he don't!" he said, and glanced at his friend. "We know why he's here! He snuck off Echo Creek Reservation and wants us to buy him whiskey. Ain't that right, Antelope Piss?"

The other white man laughed at the name but the Indian continued to stare at them, apparently unseeing.

"I don't like the look in his eyes," the smaller one said.

"And I don't like what's going on here," Spur said.

The two men spun at his voice and stared hard at Spur, who held his Colt loosely.

"Why the hell not? You an injun lover?" the acne scarred man asked.

"Hell no. But there's no law that says you have to shoot Navajos just because they're off the reservation."

"Who the hell are you? Where's your star?"

"Get out of here and leave him alone."

"I don't like nobody telling me what to do," the tall man said. "But I do like these odds. Two to one. Think we can win?" he asked his companion.

"I said, leave. Now!"

As the man glanced at his friend Spur kicked the gun from his hand and then pushed him toward the stocky man. The second lost his aim and Spur quickly held his revolver to the shorter one's neck. "Holster your weapon or your brains'll be scattered all over this alley." Spur's voice was tight. He glanced at the tall man, who stood holding his hand. He wasn't moving toward the Colt that lay on the ground.

"You sonofabitch!" he said.

"Do it!" Spur said, jabbing the barrel against fatboy's throat.

He holstered the weapon. Spur smiled and nodded pleasantly to them. "Now get the hell out of here."

The blotchy faced one reached down for his gun.

"You can get it later, when me and the Indian are gone. Move your butts!" he shouted.

They ran off.

"I'll be back!" the tall one shouted over his shoulder.

Spur turned to the Indian, who still leaned against the brick wall. The man's lips parted and Spur saw the hint of a smile.

"Thank you," the Indian said in English.

"I'd suggest you leave Hanging Rocks," Spur said.

The Indian nodded wearily and moved toward the edge of town as Spur headed off to find Leon Fairfax.

100

TEN

"Colby, what the hell's going on here?" Stanton asked as he looked at his half-dressed daughter and his employee, who stood in his underwear.

"It wasn't rape," he said. "I never touched her."

Stanton looked hard at Caroline. "Is that true?"

She nodded. "I don't know why I said that; it just seemed like the right thing."

"Thanks a lot, Caroline!"

"You shut up, Colby! Get dressed, both of you, and be in my office in two minutes." He turned and, shaking his head, walked out of Caroline's bedroom.

"Jesus, Caroline!" Colby said, pulling up his pants. "Why'd you say that? You could've gotten me killed!"

She giggled. "Maybe because I wished you *had* raped me. At least then I'd have something to show for our time together." Caroline turned to slip into her dress.

Colby knew she was joking. "Never mind." He sat on her bed to pull on his boots.

"Mr. Colby!" she said, shocked, as she turned around.

He jumped. "What? Where?"

"Please don't sit on my bed. My father might get the wrong idea."

Colby smiled and sank down again, pulling on his boots. "You've got some sense of humor, Caroline."

She giggled.

"Just you wait, little lady. There'll be another time. I'll get you in bed yet."

She smiled and finished dressing, then sat in a rattan chair and pushed her feet into high topped shoes. "We'll see about that! Now come on, we've got to see father and let him yell at us for a while." She shook her head. "He seems to be doing a lot of that lately, doesn't he?"

"I hadn't noticed." Colby fumbled over the knot on his boot and tried again.

"I think he's up to something—planning something." Caroline looked at him as she waited impatiently. "Do you know what my father's doing?"

He concentrated on the laces. "No."

Caroline sighed. "We'll talk about it later. Now we've got to go downstairs."

He finished and they walked quickly to the office that sat at the front of the house. After knocking they heard a curt "Enter!"

The office had huge windows on two sides that looked out on a magnificent view of the red rocks and dazzling sky outside, but Colby's eyes were drawn to the man seated behind the impressive desk.

Stanton frowned, arms crossed on his chest, a smoking cheroot dangling from his lips.

"Mr. Stanton, I—"

"Shut up, Colby," he said. "I am not a stupid man. I'm somewhat old-fashioned, but not stupid. It was obvious you weren't raping Caroline, no

102

matter what she said—and by the way, that was quite thoughtless of you, Caroline! What I *can't* understand is why you were standing there with your prick hanging out—forgive me, Caroline—and both of you dressed in your underclothing, not touching each other, not writhing on the bed!''

"We were staying cool," Colby said. "That's why Caroline said she took off her dress."

"It didn't look like you were cool," Stanton said, then dismissed Colby from his gaze. "Young lady," he said, turning toward his daughter, "I realize you're not as innocent as I once thought, but there is a time and a place for everything, and bed matters are done at night. If you have to romance my maintenance man away from his work at least wait until dark!"

She nodded meekly, astonished at his words.

"And as for you, Colby, well, hell, women are she-devils and tempters, and Caroline is no exception. She's got a lot of her mother in her, rest her soul, so I don't blame you or Caroline for that matter. But I will not walk into a scene like that again in this house. Understood?"

"Yes, Mr. Stanton."

"Now get out of here—both of you! I've got to go over these damned payroll records."

"Thank you, father," Caroline said.

They stole from the office and closed the door. Caroline looked at Colby and smiled. She suddenly embraced him, pushed her body against his, and leaned her head back, lips parted.

Colby pressed his mouth onto hers, his tongue thrashing, probing while she ground her hips against him.

She broke the kiss and smiled at him again, then released Colby and pushed his arms off.

"Later," she whispered. "Maybe tonight when he's sleeping." She put a hand on his crotch. "That's gonna be mine!" Caroline said, then walked to the stairs.

"Women!" Colby wiped his mouth and frowned.

Margaret Bishop tucked her red hair into a black bonnet, drew her shawl about her shoulders, and left her house to walk to the carriage and the freckle faced boy who had brought it to her house.

"Good afternoon, Matt."

"Afternoon, Miss Bishop. I hope I'm not late. I had to brush down two horses before I could come today."

"Not at all. Thank you." She allowed the boy to help her into the carriage, and once seated he handed her the reins. Margaret promptly held out a quarter for the boy.

"Thank *you!*" he said and ran off to his father and the livery stable.

Margaret smiled nervously as she drove out of town north, toward the forest. This was her regular weekly ride, and she looked forward to it more each week. It was her time to leave the civilized niceties of Hanging Rocks and explore the primitive, natural aspects of life.

At the Crooked Trail Margaret turned her carriage right toward Cottonwood Creek, travelling through a forest of those trees and junipers where runoff from the surrounding mountains provided the moisture necessary for their growth. The sun sparkled and blinked above her through the trees as she rode unhurriedly toward her special, private spot, where no one would ever see.

The horse responded well. This new beast Matt

had brought today seemed fine, gentle. Though it did make her a bit nervous to know how much energy and strength was contained in the animal, she was dependent on it and relaxed as much as possible.

She knew she was early, for she'd glanced at the Seth-Thomas on the mantel just before Matt had arrived with the carriage. So she let the horse amble along the barely distinguishable track through the trees, following the river which sparkled beside her.

After a half hour Margaret gently turned the horse off the trail around a twisted juniper tree and into a thicket of brush. There she tied the horse to a tree where it could forage and drink from the stream and walked into the bushes. As she pushed through them their leafy branches slid off her body harmlessly—no barbs or thorns on them, she had learned from past trips.

Eventually she moved beyond the last few shrubs and entered a nearly circular clearing, with flat ground lying bare of any vegetation except soft, green grass. Margaret smoothed her hair as she stood within the clearing, safe in her sanctuary, Hanging Rocks far behind her.

A noise in front of her made Margaret start. She looked into the bushes tensely, taking a step forward. After more rustling the six-foot high undergrowth of stunted trees and shrubs parted to reveal a tall, muscled Navajo man, his feet wrapped in moccasins, a scant loincloth covering his crotch.

Margaret looked at the man for a second, then stumbled forward. The Indian grabbed her and held her close while Margaret buried her face against his hairless chest, inhaling the sharp, familiar scent of his sweat.

"Running Bear!" she said ecstatically.

The Indian's powerful arms squeezed her against him while he smelled her hair and one hand reached down to cup her soft buttocks. As he pushed against her Margaret felt his arousal.

He released her and she pressed her mouth to Running Bear's, knowing that it didn't particularly arouse him but that he would do it to please her. She tasted him and pulled her head away.

"I've missed you," she said, stepping back to look at the handsome man, his muscles rippling beneath his shining red skin. Running Bear's face was strong, masculine yet gentle. His brown eyes and unruly black hair made him mysterious to Margaret's eyes.

Now she reached over to untie his loincloth but his hands stopped her.

"First, you," he said.

Margaret shivered at his voice, then his touch as his calloused hands undressed her gently. He laid each garment as he removed it on the soft leaved bushes. When she was naked he produced a blanket which he spread on the ground.

She laid on it timidly and stared up at the huge Indian, remembering how they'd first met as he looked hungrily at her. His front flap rose steadily from the pressure under it as Margaret thought back.

She had been out on a ride through the forest on a particularly hot day, since she knew it was usually cooler under the trees beside the cold water stream. Since no breeze blew among the tree trunks, however, Margaret found herself hotter still, and so she had stopped the carriage in a secluded spot, slipped off her clothing, then stepped into the stingingly cold Cottonwood Creek.

She'd almost shouted at the chill but Margaret soon felt her body adjust. She walked into the water until it reached her waist, held up her hair, and ducked down, immersing herself almost to her chin.

The water was deliciously cold and she remained in it for fifteen minutes. Almost forgetting her surroundings, Margaret walked out of the river, the water running off her magnificently formed body in sparkling drops. She sighed and turned to her clothing—and saw a naked Indian man, his hand wrapped around the huge erection that jutted out before him.

It was a moment before Margaret could respond to the man's sudden appearance. "Stay away from me!" she'd shouted, but the Indian smiled.

"I no hurt," he said.

She was startled. "You speak English?" She draped one hand over her breasts, poorly concealing the huge globes, and the other over her bush.

"Yes. Army taught me."

"You—you shouldn't do things like that," she said, waving a finger.

The Indian didn't seem to understand. "Do what?" he asked, still stroking, then smiled. 'You mean this?" He lewdly thrust his hips forward, sliding his penis through his encircled fingers.

Margaret screamed and covered her eyes, revealing her body. "Yes, that!"

"Why?"

"Why?" She didn't look at him. "It's a sin. God said it was a sin."

"Which god? Not one of mine."

She removed her hands and opened her eyes, then reluctantly looked at him. Margaret was

107

fascinated by the rhythm he built up while gazing at her body. When she looked at his eyes he smiled and Margaret was captivated. This was no ignorant savage. His eyes were all-knowing, and as she looked at him Margaret Bishop knew she desired him.

He's an Indian, she thought viciously, continuing to look hungrily at him. A dirty, filthy, heathen Indian! The thoughts crossed her mind but didn't jell; they were other people's thoughts, not hers.

Since her husband Edgar had died ten years ago she hadn't seen a naked man, hadn't made love. After a decade of torment and bittersweet memories of clutching bodies and incredible pleasures, she stared at the naked Indian pulling on himself before her without the slightest hint of shyness.

She then took a step forward, toward him, lowering her gaze to his busy hand. Then three more steps. In moments she stood before him, naked as he was, unashamed.

"Do you want me?"

The Indian had nodded.

Margaret frowned. Though she couldn't look at it while doing so Margaret took his organ in her hand, gasped at its heat and size, and rubbed it gently. The Indian groaned steadily and jerked his hips toward her fist as his foreskin slid back and forth. He touched her breast and then ran another hand down to her vee, where he probed into her with a large finger.

Margaret's eyes flooded as she felt the old sensations again, the shivers and sparks. She smiled happily and didn't protest as he laid her arms around his neck, wrists crossed, and lifted her by her waist, pressing her bottom against his hairless thighs. She locked her ankles around him to keep from slipping down.

The Indian man lifted her higher, then slowly lowered Margaret onto his enormous member. Margaret's body shook as he entered her.

After that first chance meeting, Margaret had arranged to meet Running Bear every week in the same place.

Now as he stood above her and untied his loincloth, revealing the same manhood she remembered and loved, Margaret knew her actions that day hadn't been foolish and stupid. Running Bear was no savage; he was intelligent, honest, willing to please her and one of the finest human beings she'd ever met!

Yes, he's an Indian, Margaret had thought a thousand times since, usually at night when she couldn't sleep for want of his warm body beside her, but that didn't matter. She didn't care what her race thought of the Navajo. Running Bear was her lover, and if she could have it her way she'd live with him.

Now the Indian, his light copper body glistening with sweat in the sun, knelt over her, his knees straddling her head, and lowered his mouth to her crotch as she raised hers toward his turgid penis.

Running Bear parted her nether lips, tongued the opening and clitoris and gently bit. Margaret groaned as she opened her mouth and his organ slid down. She choked but didn't pull back as he fully penetrated her. She caressed his testicles as he pulled out, gave her time to breathe, then rammed home again.

Margaret continued to shiver with pleasure as they stimulated each other. Running Bear lapped between her legs with fervor, then suddenly lifted himself from her and turned around. He grabbed Margaret and pulled her onto her side, then lifted one of her legs and slid into position. He pushed his groin until it pressed against hers and moved so that their bodies became a giant x with their crotches the point marking the center.

Running Bear squeezed her breasts with one hand as he plunged into her. Margaret sighed and her eyes widened as she felt his body enter hers. She reached out to touch his powerful, pagan face, infused with lust and an almost religious fervor.

He began the incredible thrusting to which she had grown accustomed, pounding her body so hard she knew she'd ache in the morning. But he thrilled her with climax after climax, sometimes plunging a finger in beside his penis to manually stimulate her clit. Running Bear also moved her body into exciting positions which allowed him to penetrate her at various angles, creating unending and exciting variety.

After fifteen minutes of vigorous pumping Running Bear's face contorted. His body shook and sweat poured from him as he shot his seed into her, gazing at Margaret and holding her head as he ejaculated.

Running Bear shook and grunted through his pleasure, stimulating Margaret to one last peak before they both lay shivering on the blanket.

He rubbed her breast with his nose and pulled her closer then started to withdraw.

"No!" she said, shoving forward, firmly lodging him within her. "I want it up there forever!"

Running Bear laughed and ran a hand along her shoulder. "You are wild, free, Margaret," his voice still guttural with excitement.

"You make me *feel* wild, Running Bear, when-

110

ever I'm near you. But when I'm alone—I get lonely at night."

He didn't speak, but pulled her closer, cradling his body around hers so that they didn't lose their intimate connection.

"I know. It is impossible."

"Why?" she demanded. "It can't be. We can go somewhere, live in a place where they don't care."

The Indian frowned. "They care everywhere."

"Damn them!" Margaret said, tears threatening. "Damn them all!"

He nosed her hair as she fought breaking down and touched his right nipple.

"Running Bear, I love you. You know that."

He was silent.

"I can't take this—seeing you once a week for a few hours. I'll go crazy. I'm always worried you won't be there—and I'm afraid we'll be caught."

"I've found a new place," he said.

She looked at him eagerly. "Where?"

"Not far from here. Much safer. I can come two times a week."

Margaret squeezed inside around his penis, still firm though motionless. "That would be wonderful!"

He smiled. "Yes." Running Bear thrust into her with short movements. "No more talk."

Running Bear kissed her as Margaret closed her eyes and thrilled to his plunging. She wrapped her arms around him and listened to his heartbeat as her Indian lover pumped her to ecstasy, not giving a damn what the good folk of Hanging Rocks would think.

ELEVEN

A rivulet of sweat slid into Spur's eye. He wiped his hand across his forehead, sending glistening drops flying as he walked down the unshaded boardwalk on Broad Street in Hanging Rocks.

Leon Fairfax ambled a half block down, his steps unsure due to his previous hour in the Longbar Saloon.

Spur had been watching the man for two hours. He'd sat three tables away from him in the saloon, listening in on his conversation. Although he did mention Indians several times, and his hatred of them, it didn't seem uppermost on his mind. Instead, Spur heard again and again about the tribulations of going on a seven day drunk.

Soon Fairfax had wasted another half hour looking into dusty shop windows. Spur grew restless, crossed the street and sat on a bench outside the post office.

Ten minutes later Fairfax moved off Broad Street and Spur, following, quickly saw Margaret Bishop's house directly before him as they walked down the street. Instead of going there, however, Fairfax moved to a huge two story house across the intersection of Oak and Second. Spur remembered seeing the massive brick structure as he'd accompanied Margaret to her home.

Now Fairfax disappeared into it after waiting briefly on the porch. Spur figured it might be a good time to visit Margaret. She would know who lived in the place.

He knocked and the door quickly swung open.

"Why Mr. McCoy! What a pleasant surprise!" Margaret smiled, though a bit nervously. She held a feather duster.

"I hope I'm not disturbing you, ma'am," Spur said, removing his hat.

"Not at all. Please, come in."

Spur glanced behind him at the house and walked inside.

"I'm dusting," she said, indicating the feather topped tool. "What brings you here?"

"I was wondering who lived across the street, in that huge brick house.

Margaret's face fell. "That's Michael Stanton and his weird *family.*" She shook her head. "I've never known quite what to think of them. They're strange."

"How?"

She looked at him briefly. "Well, for instance, Mr. Stanton must be forty or so, an old war hero, and he's got his eighteen year old daughter Caroline living with him. Then there's that David Colby fellow. He stays there too."

"Is this Stanton a good man?"

"I don't know if I'd say good; he's rich. Owns half of Hanging Rocks, even the church! Michael Stanton is certainly the richest man around here." She shook her head. "Why?"

Spur shrugged. "I was just wondering, because of the size of the house, I guess."

She looked at Spur as if she were trying to make up her mind, then folded her hands before her. "Mr. McCoy, why did you come to Hanging Rocks?"

"I—I beg your pardon, Mrs. Bishop?"

Margaret laughed. "I may be a woman but I'm not stupid. You asked me about the massacres the last time we talked. Is that why you've come here? Are you investigating them?"

Spur hesitated. He didn't want the good folk of Hanging Rocks to know his mission. But he felt he could trust the lonely woman. He nodded.

"I thought so!" Margaret said, delighted.

"But I can't tell you more."

"Oh, I don't care about that. I knew I was right." She laid a finger on her chin. "And why are you asking about the Stanton House?"

"Business," he said and smiled.

Margaret looked frankly at him. "Something to do with the ranching families who were killed? Some connection?"

Spur was silent.

"Mr. McCoy, aren't you forgetting something?" Her voice was faintly sarcastic. "Everyone *knows* the Navajo killed them. If you're looking for the man who murdered the MacDonalds and the Goodnights you should be looking at the reservation!"

"I remember what you said the last time we talked. You said something about how *they should all know*. Know what?"

Margaret turned from him and stared at the wall. "Know better," she said, and sighed.

"That's what I'm beginning to think."

"Really?" She was pleased.

Spur shook his head. "Just a feeling. If they didn't do it, if the Indians didn't who did?"

115

She held out her hand. "I don't know. I can't think of a reason. The Goodnights and Mac-Donalds almost never came to town, they kept pretty much to themselves. Maybe once a month we'd see old Ray MacDonald, but that was about all. I can't understand why anyone would want to kill them."

"That's what's making folks here in Hanging Rocks think the Navajo did it," Spur said evenly. "But there is—can be—another reason. I think someone killed them and deliberately made it look like the Navajo had done it."

She looked at him curiously. "Really? What makes you say that?"

"I looked over their ranches; that's what the signs point to. Of course, I can't be sure."

"Are you looking around town for the men who killed them?"

He nodded.

"And that's why you were asking about the Stanton place? You don't think he killed them, do you?"

Spur shook his head. "No, no. I've never heard of him before. I was following another man and he went into Stanton's house." Spur moved to the door and looked out the lace curtains. Fairfax was walking down the street.

"I've got to leave," Spur said, turning back to her. "Listen, Mrs. Bishop. Could I come back here and watch the Stanton house again if I need to?"

"Of course," she said. "I wouldn't mind at all. Not if you think it'll help you find the real murderers, the ones who're blaming the Navajo."

"Thank you, Mrs. Bishop. You're a real lady."

She beamed. "Thank *you*, Mr. McCoy."

He rushed from the house and, closing the door behind him, strode quickly toward Broad Street.

Fairfax had already disappeared from view.

As he walked he was struck by a thought. Margaret had mentioned Stanton's daughter—*Caroline.* Eighteen years old, she'd said. Was that the same Caroline who'd snuck into his room and whom he'd bedded? Spur laughed. Could be. Anything is possible in a small town.

When he turned onto Broad Street, Spur couldn't locate Fairfax. He crisscrossed the street several times, dodging wagons, carriages and groups of mounted men, but didn't see Fairfax again.

Cursing, he turned toward Sheriff Hughes' office. Spur found the man breaking down a rifle and oiling it.

"Hughes, what's the story on this Michael Stanton?"

The sheriff looked up in surprise. "Stanton? A fine man. Owns a lot of land and some gold and silver mines. He's worth more than all the other residents of Hanging Rocks put together; practically owns the town. Why?"

"Just wondering."

"How you coming with the Navajos?" he asked. "You found the ones who did it yet?"

Spur was silent.

"No? Well, then hell, might as well just pick out two or three of them, kill them to warn the real murderers, and let them take the blame." Hughes looked up at Spur. "Isn't that right?"

"Hell no, Hughes!" Spur kicked the man's desk, pushing it four inches toward Hughes. Its sharp edge pressed against the lawman's stomach.

"Christ, McCoy!" Hughes said, shoving it away from him. "I was only kidding."

"Goddamn you! I'll have you locked up in one of your own cells if you don't shape up and start acting like a sheriff!''

"What'd I do?" he asked. "Hell, they're just Indians!''

"They're human beings.''

"Maybe, but they're not U.S. citizens. That means they haven't got any rights here. I know the law and I know that Indians are kind of like cattle.''

Spur withheld the punch he was ready to throw and stepped back. "You know what I think?''

"What?" Hughes had placed the rifle on the table and looked at Spur cautiously.

"I think there's something wrong here in Hanging Rocks. And you know about it.''

"What the hell are you talking about?" Hughes said. "Christ, I think something's wrong with *you*, McCoy! You an Indian lover or something? It figures—the government sent in an Indian lover to find out which Navajos killed my people!" Hughes shook his head. "That sounds like the government.''

"I don't hate the Indians just because their skin is darker," Spur said. "Is this whole town crazy or what? It'd be different if they'd been raiding you, attacking you, but as far as I can tell things have been quiet.''

Hughes exploded. "What about the MacDonalds and the Goodnights? They're rotting in the cemetery!''

Spur shook his head. "The Navajo didn't kill them.''

"What?" The sheriff was incredulous. "You deaf or something, McCoy? I said the Indians killed them!''

"They didn't kill them. Those ranching families were murdered by white men.''

The sheriff studied Spur for a moment, then

118

shook his head. "I don't believe you're serious."

"I am."

"Come on, McCoy. I rode out there the day it happened and looked over the ranches. Broken arrows and bows all over the place. Moccasin tracks. Arrowheads. And you say it wasn't Indians?" Hughs snorted.

"Anybody could have worn moccasins and thrown those things around. Not only have the Navajo been virtually peaceful for three years, they still are. And now their people are being killed off, probably by the same whites who massacred the ranchers to make the Navajo look bad."

"You're wrong," Hughes said. "That's the god-damndest thing I've ever heard!"

Spur ignored him. "And you're sitting there on your fat butt waiting for me to plug a few Indians so you'll look good and everyone in Hanging Rocks will be happy!"

Hughes face reddened. He started to rise and talk but Spur pushed him roughly back into his chair and cut off his words.

"Shut the fuck up, Hughes! I've heard enough of your asinine comments." McCoy walked to the door.

"Wait!"

Spur turned and looked at the man.

"I'm—I'm sorry, McCoy." The sheriff sighed. "I don't know if I believe all those things I said. I certainly didn't have anything against the Navajo when I first moved here. It's been peaceful and we haven't had any problems with them, except for the occasional Indian who buys alcohol or hunts off the reservation. That sort of thing. The army kept things quiet in the early stages, then moved out. Now a man from the Bureau of Indian Affairs goes out there once a month to Echo Creek Reservation

119

to see how they are."

"If you don't think that way why in hell are you talking like that?"

Hughes' face fell. "All the talk I hear in the saloons and on the streets, I guess."

Spur frowned.

"Everyone's jawing about the Navajos, how we should move the reservation, or drive them away by force if we can't get it done legally. In fact, I heard a few men say that the massacres were the best thing that's ever happened to Hanging Rocks, because it's finally got us to wake up to the *Indian Problem*, whatever the hell that is."

"You remember who said that?"

"Let me think." Hughes drummed his finger on the desk. "Fairfax? Stanton?"

"I thought you said Fairfax was a good man."

"He is—by our standards."

"Michael Stanton. Hmmm. If it was him—"

"What?"

"Never mind. Look, I shouldn't have to tell you to keep quiet about this, right?"

"You can count on me, McCoy, and I'm sorry I—"

"Hell, Hughes; I knew you weren't that kind of man. Otherwise I wouldn't waste my time on you."

"Thanks," the sheriff said, grinning. "And tell me what you find out."

Spur left Hughes' office and went to the hitching post outside Cicily's Hotel. Could he ride to the reservation tonight? He checked the sun, then his Waterbury. No. Too late. Dusk in an hour.

He cursed and headed for the Longbar. Maybe he could pick up some interesting local news—especially about Leon Fairfax and Michael Stanton.

TWELVE

Chief Eagle Feather stooped as he walked from the camp. The braves weren't back from hunting yet, so the camp behind him was quiet. A dog barked ceaselessly somewhere as he peered at the ground around him. Eagle Feather had to find the right cactus, in the correct spot.

Though he was quite old, the Navajo had never forgotten that he was the son of a sorcerer as well as the son of a chief. His father had gone from spells to wars nearly fifty years ago to lead the tribe to victory in skirmishes with all manner of enemies.

Before doing so he had trained his son Eagle Feather in the ways of frenzy witchcraft, eagle pit way, curing, and all the old magics of his ancestors. Eagle Feather had learned every chant, each action, the manipulation of such things as images carved of lightning-struck wood, *datura*, cactus spines, collected spittle and urine-soaked sand.

Now as he walked searching for the perfect form of the cactus, one that leaned toward the constant star, Eagle Feather ran over the information in his mind, refreshing his familiarity with it before actually putting it into practice.

He could not make a mistake.

Eagle Feather remembered how his father had told him late one night that though he had lain aside his medicine bundle for a bow and arrows, he never thought it wrong to use magic to ensure victory in battle, success in the hunt and to maintain peace in the tribe, and so Eagle Feather had finally learned how his father had been such a strong, good chief—he had used magic.

The old man spotted the right plant. Instead of approaching it directly Eagle Feather hobbled in a circle around it, ignoring the pain in his legs. As he moved he chanted an old song:

> "Going around, with it I shall return.
> Circling around, with the spine I shall return,
> The leaning cactus, with it I shall return.
> The sharp one, with it I shall return.
> The spine, with it I shall return.
> To make magic, with it I shall return.
> To set him free, with it I shall return.
> It is finished in power.
> It is finished in power."

Eagle Feather stood before the plant, which tilted to his right. He reached out a shaking hand and pushed a fleshy finger onto the topmost spine. The pain shocked him, as it always did. He stabbed harder, pressing into the plant before he took from it.

As the spine touched his finger bone the old man nearly fainted but quickly withdrew his digit. Blood shone eerily on the bright green, flattened cactus stalk. Eagle Feather ignored the pounding in his hand and removed one two-inch spine, mumbled a prayer of thanks, and turned to walk back to his hogan before he was seen.

He sucked his finger as he stared at his distant home. The chief had wandered much farther than he had planned, and he dreaded the extra steps back. Eagle Feather hurt when he walked, sat or laid still. Walking was the worst, however; it seemed that vicious insects bit his muscles as he moved them.

The old chief kept his mind on matters at hand: the spine and the spell.

He knew he had to kill Rainbow Dream to save the tribe. Even though he risked the spiritual consequences, and knew he shouldn't take life from within the tribe, there were exceptions to such codes. This was one of them.

Jaw firm against the pain, he returned home and secreted the spine within his leather bag of charms and herbs. One more item and he'd be ready.

Rainbow Dream should still be out hunting with the other men, Eagle Feather knew, so if he wanted some of the man's water he'd have to wait several hours. Then his eyes lit and a smile marred his solemn face. There were other ways . . .

The chief went outside again, his beloved orange and black striped blanket wrapped tightly around him. As he shuffled to Rainbow Dream's hogan he stroked the blanket, remembering how his first squaw had woven it for him just before she'd died in childbirth, losing the child as well.

Eagle Feather closed his eyes at the bitter, faded memory, then peered around him as he shuffled across the camp. Only a few grandmothers with screaming babies were visible; the women must have gone fishing or were out collecting wild onions and pine nuts.

He ducked into Rainbow Dream's hogan and searched it eagerly. Eagle Feather saw one small pair of moccasins and growled at them, then found a larger pair, well worn, with the distinctive beadwork design he'd seen Rainbow Dream wear.

As the chief reached down to lift them from the dirt floor he stumbled. Eagle Feather cried out as his old body hit the ground but held back another sound; he didn't want to be seen.

The chief painfully straightened up, stuffed the moccasins under his blanket out of sight and climbed to his knees.

A beautiful squaw entered the hogan and screamed as she saw him, then blushed and knelt. "I'm sorry, Chief Eagle Feather! I did not realize it was you."

He looked at her and nodded, unsmiling. "I came to see Rainbow Dream but fell down. I'm old."

"You should rest," she said, smiling and showing perfect white teeth. "Are you hurt?"

"No more than usual, Singing Jay." Eagle Feather again thought what an incongruous name Rainbow Dream's squaw had; the woman's voice was the sweetest in the tribe.

"Let me help you." She tried to grip his hands but he kept them beneath the blanket, one clutching the moccasins to his chest. The leather was cold against his skin.

"No. I'm fine." He rose unsteadily to his feet, placing one hand on the ground before him.

"Rainbow Dream is hunting," Singing Jay said.

"Why did I expect him to be here?" Eagle Feather asked, shaking his head as if senile. "I'll be back," he said, and left the woman.

As the sun hit his eyes Eagle Feather's skull seemed to split with throbbing. He hurried to his hogan and, out of breath, collapsed before the smouldering cinders.

The chief hid the moccasins under his sleeping blankets. He was ready. Now only one thing waited—nightfall.

Six hours later Rainbow Dream walked through the camp. It was quiet as always after dark. Most families were huddled in their hogans by now. He saw smoke rising from Chief Eagle Feather's, lit by the fire that created it. He walked to the hogan softly and stopped before the entrance. Peering in he saw the old chief dozing before his dying fire, sitting crosslegged, eyes closed, wrapped in his ever present blanket.

He had to kill him, Rainbow Dream told himself. Not only so that he could lead the tribe, but also to ensure that there was no opposition to the morning raid. Rainbow Dream hadn't formally announced the attack on Hanging Rocks yet but he'd heard the gossip. The men expected it.

As he ducked into the hogan Rainbow Dream slipped a knife from his breechcloth string and cautiously approached the apparently slumbering man.

His moccasin rattled a stone on the hard packed earthen floor and at the sound Eagle Feather's head snapped up. He saw Rainbow Dream and sighed.

"I knew you'd come," the chief said. "You've decided against attacking the round eyes."

Rainbow Dream laughed lowly. "No."

The chief didn't seem surprised. "If you want my approval, you won't have it. You know what I think of your plan."

"I don't want your approval." Rainbow Dream spat at Eagle Feather.

As the spittle hit his face and dripped across his

lips the chief wiped it onto his beloved blanket. "Then why are you here?" he asked simply.

Rainbow Dream's eyes narrowed as he knelt before the man, holding the knife point upward.

The chief glanced at it and nodded. "I expected that, too, Rainbow Dream."

"No. You couldn't have known!"

Eagle Feather's face cracked into a smile. "Do not forget. I am the son of a sorcerer chief."

Rainbow Dream's face flashed with the old superstitious fears, then cleared. "You don't fool me, old man!"

The chief silently spread his arms, allowing the blanket to fall from his shoulders. Rainbow Dream was shocked at the man's sunken chest, protruding ribs, and unnatural bluish skin color. He was dying.

The chief raised his hands and Rainbow Dream saw one of his moccasins in one hand, something long and sharp in the other.

"What are you doing?" he asked quickly.

Chief Eagle Feather's face was calm as he wiped the inside of the moccasin across the spittle covered blanket, then laid it on the ground before his crotch and raised the other.

It came down hard against the sole. When the chief retracted it Rainbow Dream chilled.

A cactus thorn pierced his moccasin. The old death spell.

"Die by the spine!" the old man chanted.

"No. I don't believe it!"

"Die by the spine!"

"No!" He pounded his foot against the ground; it felt good, no shooting pains, no witchcraft had invaded there. The old man's powers were false. The white man had taught him that.

"Die by the spine!"

Rainbow Dream slashed Chief Eagle Feather's left chest, leaving a wide line of red. At that moment the old man pulled a blade of his own from beneath his thigh and buried it in the brave's chest with startling strength.

Rainbow Dream screamed in terror as he felt the cold steel drive into him. His own knife fell harmlessly to the ground as he clutched at the handle that Eagle Feather still gripped.

Rainbow Dream's consciousness wavered; he saw the old man, grunting, lips moving with a war song, then all was black. The blade slipped from him as he fell backwards. Rainbow Dream had already slipped into the *otherworld* before he hit the ground.

Eagle Feather pressed his hand to the chest wound, gasping, quenching the slow trickle of blood. Rainbow Dream lay dead before him. When he felt little blood seeping out he quickly pulled the spine from the moccasin, threw it into the fire, then added wood to the blaze from the pile beside him. As the flames rose he threw the moccasins onto it. The leather sputtered and stank as it burned.

Eagle Feather reached for his medicine bundle and brought out two handfuls of sage leaves, which he scattered on the flames to sweeten the smoke. He then adjusted the loincloth, left the saliva soiled blanket on the ground, rose to his feet and went outside to rouse Singing Jay. He had to be the one to tell her.

When the old chief arrived at Rainbow Dream's hogan she was awake and staring at the entrance. After seeing Eagle Feather she bent at the waist, covered her face and wailed.

127

She knew.

There was nothing he could do. Eagle Feather shuffled back toward his hogan to wait the dawn. No need to mention the sorcery he'd practiced, unless Singing Jay noticed that her man's old pair of moccasins were missing.

As he made his way across the fire lit camp Singing Jay rushed past him, crying, and disappeared into his hogan. She emerged moments later, dragging her husband's body outside. She laid her head on his chest over the stab wound and sobbed.

Eagle Feather's stomach threatened to revolt but he stilled it. He couldn't return to his home. Rainbow Dream's spirit hovered there. He turned to the closest hogan and looked in it. Inside a young couple pleasured each other in the dim moonlight that spilled in through the opening at the roof's peak.

He sighed and sat at the large communal cooking fire, while Singing Jay's lamentations rang out and he heard grunts and sharp cries from the hogan behind him.

It was done.

THIRTEEN

"You know I don't blame you, Colby," Michael Stanton said as he poured the man a drink in his office.

"I'm glad of that sir," he said.

"She's a wild one, Caroline is. I know she's—well, she's not as pure as I'd like. So let's not talk about it again. Okay?"

Colby nodded. "Anything you say, Mr. Stanton."

"Good." He handed Colby a drink and splashed some whiskey into a glass for himself. "I think we should have another meeting tomorrow night. Now that we've lost both Buck and Cousins we're down two. I know there must be more honest men in town, men who want to be rid of the Indians and who'll do something about it!"

"There are lots of them," Colby said. "But you told them to be careful, remember? Do we have to be so secretive? I mean, it's hard to drum supporters when you're making the men approach possible members so quietly."

"You know we have to do that. Otherwise, if we're an open militia that eveeryone knows about we'd be crushed before we could gain sufficient men. The army would send troops over here from Fort Prescott and wipe us out, the dirty bastards, because they're supposed to *protect* the Indians."

"What a joke!" Colby threw in.

"I have too much to think about, too much to risk, so we'll keep quiet about the army for a month or two longer."

"What about your idea of hiring guns from Phoenix or Tucson?"

Stanton shook his head. "Too far away, and nowhere to put the men. I can't have them living in this house." He shook his head. "No. We need local men—there are three thousand people living in Hanging Rocks, for chrissakes! You'd think we could get a couple hundred together!"

"We'll do it," Colby said. "Shit, it's only been two weeks. Give it time. It'll grow."

Stanton smiled. "You're goddamned right it will!" he said. "I'm going to build Hanging Rocks the finest private army ever organized—the best dressed, most disciplined and yet vicious band of men I can get. We'll sweep across the reservation, hunting down and killing those damned savages, ever last stinking one of them!" Stanton roared.

"Yeah," Colby said.

Stanton didn't seem to notice. "Those goddamned Navajos are going to go where they belong —to hell! When we have the right number of men, with the right training, the Navajos won't stand a chance. We can organize and kill off every Navajo within a hundred miles of here, then disband before the army gets wind of us."

"Huh?" Colby asked. "I thought you said we were going to wipe the Indians out—all of them."

"Sure—the close-by ones. If we can't we'll raise such a racket the government will have to move the reservation. At least we can reduce the population on Echo Creek by half."

"And if the army don't move the reservation?" Colby asked.

"Then we'll regroup and wipe the bloodthirsty bastards out!" Stanton smiled as he sipped the whiskey. "Hell, I'll probably be a national hero, written up in the newspapers back east. They said the Indian wars were over, but they're not—the bloodiest one's going to start in a few weeks."

Colby laughed and finished his whiskey. "You talk big, Mr. Stanton. Hell, it sounds like you're really looking forward to it."

"Of course!" Stanton said. "But after all: the only good Indian is a dead Indian. You've heard that before, haven't you? I'm going to put it into practice. I made my fortune here; my roots are here, my family. I'm not going to be forced out of Hanging Rocks by some vicious Indians who want to steal our land, rape our women, and destroy our homes!" His eyes blazed. "Soon they'll be attacking the town, riding through the streets, sending in more and more reinforcements. If we're not prepared they could conceivably destroy Hanging Rocks! I'm not going to let that happen!"

"I never thought about it that way before," Colby said. "Hey, this sounds like what the army should be doing, but they won't. It'll be just like when you were in the army, right, boss?"

Stanton's gaze chilled him. "What did you say?"

Colby shook his head. "I just meant it'll be just like when you were a war hero."

Stanton's face softened. "That's right. And when the last Navajo falls dead I'm going to throw a party for this town like it's never seen."

"Hope I'm invited," Colby said.

"Of course. But that's months away. We've got lots of grueling work ahead. I'll be out hunting every day, probably—my quota is five kills a day."

Colby whistled. "That's high, boss. Too dangerous."

Stanton stared him down. "Are you telling me what to do?"

"No, sir, I just thought that if one of those Navajo got lucky and killed you—"

"They won't!" Stanton screamed, his face red, cords standing out on his neck. "I'll kill them before they know I'm there! Christ almighty, Colby; sometimes I feel I have the power of God! If I decide some fuckin' Indian's going to die, he does. Every time! Just like the last trip we went on. Remember?"

"Yeah," Colby said with a grin. "Hey, are the uniforms in?"

Stanton nodded. "I picked them up this morning; they came in this morning on the stage. Two dozen this shipment."

"Can I see them?" Colby asked.

"No. Not yet. I think you'll find them—surprising!" The subject change seemed to have calmed Stanton.

"What do they look like?"

"You'll see. Now leave me. Take your drink with you."

"Right." Colby left the office and scratched his armpit as he stood in the hall. What had Stanton done? Copied U.S. army uniforms?

Caroline passed by. She winked but kept on moving.

Three hours after dawn Spur drew his horse to a stop on a ridge and gazed at the land before him.

Ten miles from Hanging Rocks he looked out over the sprawling stretch of Echo Creek Reservation lands.

Its namesake ran through the heart of the countryside, as did four other streams, two of which went dry during the hottest summer months, while the others were year round gushers.

Peering through the haze of hundreds of fires, Spur saw five camps scattered over the area, several miles distant from each other. Most consisted of no more than twenty or thirty dwellings each. Though the Navajo had been contained, pushed onto this corner of Arizona territory, they clung to the old ways of life as far as possible. They didn't build white men's cities.

The closest camp seemed to be the largest, so perhaps it housed the most important chief. There seemed to have been little work done to improve or maintain the land by the white men; but the hand of the Indian was everywhere evident, in the orderly fields of beans, corn and squash, a few orchards, irrigation ditches to keep the plants alive, and the trademark of the Navajo—the round wood and dirt homes called hogans.

Spur walked the horse down the cliff, figuring he'd have already been spotted. Although the Navajo were friendly, they thought of the reservation as their own country, and wanted no visitors. He wondered how much more of the vast expanse of land would be taken from them in the next ten years, as mineral deposits were discovered.

He rode through a thick forest of pines for several minutes, finally reaching its end. Just after he'd cleared the last trees he saw five riders approaching. The Indians, dressed in jeans and shirts, halted ten feet from where Spur had stopped his stallion.

"Friend," Spur said in Navajo, eyeing the quintet closely. They weren't much to look at—short, undernourished, with rotting teeth and bleary eyes. The reservation didn't seem to be a healthy place to live.

Only one of the men was healthy, with glossy hair and fiery eyes. He sat astride a beautiful white mare, a blanket for a saddle. The man looked at Spur, frowning, scratching his thigh.

"Friend," Spur said again in Navajo.

"I am Running Bear. Why come here, white man?" The power of his thickly accented voice matched that of his gaze.

If this wasn't the chief he should be, Spur thought as he wondered where the man had learned to speak English.

"I came to talk," Spur said.

Running Bear smiled. "We had many words, many promises. Now this is all we have." Running Bear gestured to the land behind him. "You are not welcome."

Spur frowned. If the Navajo would not be friendly he'd miss an important source of information. As he pondered this another rider pounded up, stopping beside Running Bear.

When the Indian turned his head Spur grinned. It was one of the men he'd met on his trip to Hanging Rocks. The Indian spoke rapidly to Running Bear.

Spur couldn't understand the words, but a moment later both Indians turned to him.

"Crooked Finger tells me you are good. You believe round eyes is killing my people, and killed whites on the *rancheros*?"

Spur nodded.

134

Running Bear lifted his chin slightly. "Come. We will talk."

With the other men surrounding him Spur rode the mile or so to camp. He dismounted with the braves and was the object of curiosity by the people, who gathered as he was escorted to the exterior of what he assumed was the chief's hogan.

An elderly Navajo appeared from the structure, stooped, his face lined with age and hair white as fresh snow. His eyes were alert and Spur felt he was being summed up as the Indian looked at him.

Running Bear spoke with the chief as Spur stood in silence, not understanding a word. When the talk ended, he was invited to sit beside the chief's fire in his hogan. When all seven men were seated the chief introduced himself as Eagle Feather, then the others in turn: Running Bear, Crooked Finger, Lame Deer—Spur quickly lost track of their names.

"Your name," Running Bear asked.

"McCoy."

"Makkoi," Eagle Feather decided, was the correct way to pronounce it.

Running Bear threw wood on the fire, crackling dry branches with the leaves and bark removed to make a nearly smokeless fire.

"Makkoi, white man kill families on *rancheros,*" Eagle Feather said. Running Bear began to interrupt but the chief waved him off and continued. "Find him, we cannot. Every scout killed or useless. Find him *you* must!"

"That's why I'm here," he said. "Can you help me?"

The chief looked to Running Bear, who apparently translated. "No. You know what we know."

"This is the same man who killed the Navajo family not long ago?" he asked hesitantly. "And the other Indians?"

Chief Eagle Feather's eyes didn't change until after Running Bear began rendering the words into Navajo. The chief slapped the man's chest before he finished the sentence to silence him. "Yes."

Spur was silent.

"No more talk," the chief said wearily.

Spur rose with the other men and was led outside. Running Bear accompanied him to his horse, then laid his hand on Spur's shoulder as he prepared to mount.

"Wait. Walk with me," the Indian said.

Spur, jolted by the contact and the suggestion, nodded and led the horse from the camp while walking beside the Indian.

"It was best you left," he said. "My people don't love your people."

Spur pulled back the corners of his mouth. "Not surprising."

"We need your help," Running Bear said, looking to the woods ahead.

"All I know is that some white man is killing whites and Indians. I don't know who's doing it."

"But you will," Running Bear said in a neutral voice.

"Hope so. That's why I came here."

They had passed the last hogans and walked onto the dusty, ill-used trail that led to Hanging Rocks. Running Bear stopped suddenly and looked at Spur.

"My people were almost killed this morning. All of them."

The Secret Service man halted and looked at Running Bear. "How?"

136

"One brave tried to kill Eagle Feather. Wanted to lead braves into battle. Attack Hanging Rocks at dawn."

Spur thought that over. "What stopped him?"

Running Bear smiled. "Chief Eagle Feather is old, but full of wise. He killed Rainbow Dream last night."

Spur almost smiled at the image of the ancient man murdering a man a third of his age, but didn't doubt Running Bear's sincerity. Why would he lie? "That was fortunate for you."

"Yes. But it may come again, this feeling for war. If I was chief, I—I'd—"

"What?"

Running Bear shook his head in frustration and started walking again. "I cannot find words, not your words."

Spur knew it was a lie but let it pass as he caught up with the man, still leading his stallion.

"You must stop this man. If more Navajo die, all Navajo will die. I will not allow!"

"What makes you think I can do it?" Spur asked.

"Nothing. I know nothing of you," he said pointedly, staring at Spur over his shoulder. "But Makkoi, we can ask no one else. You alone." The man increased his pace.

"Why do you know English so well?" Spur asked, remembering that nearly all Navajo knew little English or Spanish.

Running Bear didn't look at him. "I had white friend—I was taught. And the government man talks to me when he comes."

"I see." Spur looked at the Indian and they lasped into silence. There seemed to be something more he wanted to tell him but couldn't find the

137

courage.

McCoy was struck by the alien world the Indians lived in—not only to the whites, but to the Navajo themselves. Their old ways of living, religion and culture were dying, and they had been forced to adapt to new laws and to make marks on paper that were supposed to mean something. They were a people from a broken reality; the whites had cracked it apart.

But Running Bear wasn't the same as the rest of his people; he seemed to think differently. The man was certainly powerful, a force among the Navajo.

The tall Indian stopped and turned to Spur. "I will walk with you longer," he said.

Spur nodded.

They spoke little as they moved, and Spur continued to feel that Running Bear wasn't saying everything. He wondered if he had information about the man who was killing the Navajo or something that might be damaging to their tribe. Perhaps it was someone they'd tormented, or robbed, or harassed.

Spur knew he couldn't openly ask that question —Running Bear was sure to take offense. He had to be subtle.

"Running Bear?" he asked.

The man turned to him and grunted.

"Why do you walk with me?"

He frowned and stared at the trees ahead. "To talk."

"Do you want to say something else?"

The man shook his head.

They approached the woods, and Spur realized something. "You're off reservation lands," he said gently.

Running Bear smiled. "I am safe. Here I am

safe. There—" he pointed to the woods, "—I am not safe. There the white man kills my people. There must I go."

Spur looked at him skeptically. "Why? If it's dangerous?"

Running Bear laughed. "Chief Eagle Feather needs a plant that grows only there. I go."

They walked in silence until they reached the forest.

Running Bear turned to Spur, his face dark. "Find him, Makkoi."

Spur smiled as the Indian moved off through the rolling land studded with trees and shrubs.

FOURTEEN

Michael Stanton and Dave Colby moved slowly toward the trees, walking their mounts to make as little noise as possible. They didn't want to warn any Indians who might be in the area.

Colby smiled. Stanton had decided to go hunting again this afternoon. He figured it was probably due to the man's frustrations with his army plans, since things were going so slow. Colby was glad, whatever the man's reasons.

Not that he hadn't gone out shooting several times on his own, but Stanton seemed to know where the Indians would be with surprising accuracy, and that made it all the more fun. More targets.

Colby didn't care about the Navajo one way or the other. He'd heard the talk that they weren't really human, but he didn't think about it. He was simply following orders from Stanton. Besides, Colby liked it. He could tell his grandchildren about Indian fighting, if he ever hooked up with a woman and lived that long.

Stanton peered around them as they entered the dense forest. Colby knew the reservation wasn't more than a mile away. Actually, no one seemed to know its exact boundaries, but by common consent the forest was considered to be off the reservation. Not that anyone had bothered looking it up.

The Navajos went there often, Colby thought as he and Stanton rode past eight-foot tall junipers and higher pines. The carpet of dead needles cushioning their horses' hooves. The Indians hunted, fished the Silver Stream, gathered wild foods and did god-only-knows what else, Colby thought. Each time they found Indians in the forest they seemed to be doing something else.

"Stanton," Colby said.

"What?"

"Where are they?" he asked excitedly.

"Shut up, asshole!" Stanton said. "Not so loud!"

Colby grimaced. "Sorry."

His boss shook his head. "Want to scare them away?"

"No."

"Then keep your goddamned mouth shut!"

Colby frowned and rode beside Stanton, watching the trees. The alternating areas of shadow and bright sunlight tricked his eyes, as always; it was hard to distinguish a tree trunk from an Indian.

Stanton held up his hand, a silent signal to stop. He stepped off his horse quietly, tied her to a nearby tree, waited until Colby had done so, then moved forward. Brilliant sunshine blinded him to the darker areas, so Colby followed Stanton by a slightly circuitous route, moving from shade to shade.

As he made one of these moves Colby was startled to see a Navajo walking five hundred feet to his right. He was a tall man, and he seemed to be wandering aimlessly, head down, staring at the ground.

Probably on a drunk, Colby thought. He should tell Stanton, unless his boss was on another Indian's trail. Colby frowned, debated going to Stanton, who had by now disappeared into the woods, then shook his head and followed the Indian with his eyes, motionless. The wind rustled through the trees, stirring the branches overhead and creating background noise.

Colby moved toward the Indian, thought again and turned toward Stanton's last position. "Damn!" he said aloud. Stanton was gone.

He raced back to his original location. The Indian was out of sight. He moved slowly, passed trees and a few clumps of a silver green plant that sent off a fragrance as he brushed past them. Then he saw him.

The Indian bent over a plant, and slid a knife across its base just at the roots. Indians did strange things, he thought. They're grubbers—they even dig up wild plants and eat them.

Colby stood and watched him for a moment, then when another breeze picked up moved closer. He was fifty feet from the man when the rustling of the pines halted too soon. The Indian didn't look at him. He ran.

"Holy shit!" Colby said, fumbling with his weapon as the Navajo disappeared into the woods. He scrambled after him, cursing his impatience. Stanton always seemed in control. He never ruined a good shot.

Colby ran, dodging trees and saplings thrusting up from the forest floor, desperately searching for the Indian. He caught a flash of cloth to his right—

the Indian must have moved. He veered to that direction and heard someone crashing through the woods in front of him.

"Stop, you goddamned heathen!" he muttered, frustrated. The Navajos were excellent runners—once they started moving they didn't seem to stop.

"Shit!" Colby repeated.

Pine needles whipped his face and hands as he hurried through the brush. He again saw the man before him, long enough to fire at the moving target. He missed.

"Jeezus!" The word came from the brush before him.

Colby froze. "Who's that?" he called.

"You fuckin' idiot! If you weren't such a lousy shot you would have killed me!"

Colby blanched but kept on running. "Mr. Stanton?" he called.

"You're goddamned right it's Mr. Stanton!" he roared above the thrashing noises. "And Mr. Stanton's going to break your goddamned neck after I kill me this Navajo!"

"I'm sorry, Mr. —"

"No time for that," Stanton said, still ahead of him. "Just stop shooting at me, for chrissakes!"

Colby slowed. He knew they were nearing the end of the forest. Stanton suddenly dashed into view as he darted to the right, obviously following the Indian as he detoured to avoid leaving the relative safety of the woods.

He moved toward the again invisible Stanton, jogging, feeling his legs ache and his stomach knot. He wasn't in the best shape. Colby decided he liked hunting on horseback better.

Abruptly the noises before him stopped. Colby rushed toward the spot and saw Stanton standing, staring down, his six-shooter trained on something on the ground.

The Navajo.

Colby chuckled. "Hell, sure am glad that you didn't get away," he said.

"No thanks to you."

The Navajo, still alive, glared up at Stanton. His right leg was twisted at an unnatural angle. He must have fractured the limb in a fall over a log, Colby thought.

"You are white man who kills my people," the Indian said in an accusing voice.

Stanton looked astonished, then turned to Colby. "Hell, these damned heathens are getting smarter all the time. Now you can train them to talk! I might keep one as a pet, if only they didn't *stink* so bad."

Colby laughed raucously while the Indian continued to gaze at Stanton. "He's got that look in his eye—the one that says he knows he's finished," Colby said after guffawing.

"Yeah," Stanton said.

"Why are you killing my people?" the Indian asked.

"Goddamn! He's got all kinds of tricks, doesn't he?"

"Indeed," Stanton said. "Too bad I don't have time for them. Your shot back there's bound to bring more of his kind."

"I should have known," the Indian said. "You kill me on the ground, lamed. Should I turn my back before you shoot?"

Stanton's upper lip curled. "What the hell did you say, injun?"

He remained silent.

"Hey, boss, I wouldn't let him talk that way to

145

you!"

"Are you calling me a coward?" Stanton asked.

The Indian smiled. "You shoot women and children—babies. Shoot through the back, unarmed men. What you think?"

"You goddamn fuckin' redman!" Stanton screamed.

"You dead soon. In spirit world I find you."

"Blast him, boss!" Colby said, practically shouting, frantic. "Don't let him jabber that bullshit!"

"Stay out of this, Colby!" he said, then looked at the fallen man. "You're trying to talk me into letting you go," he said incredulously.

"No. I am not stupid." The Indian frowned. "I just want—want to—" Tears flowed from his eyes.

"The goddamned injun's bawling!" Colby said.

"One more word outa you and you'll be a gelding before dusk!" Stanton thundered to Colby.

"Kill me, coward." The Indian stared up at him.

Stanton shook his head. "Goddamn smart-ass Indian!" He sent three bullets through the man's heart.

The Indian slumped down, his head rolled to the side, as his lips seemed to form words.

"No rules in war, right?" Colby asked.

Stanton looked at him for a moment, then nodded. "Let's get the hell out of here! Those shots could bring the whole Navajo nation down on our butts!"

They ran from the area toward their horses and were soon gone, the image of the Indian with the broken leg shining vividly before Colby's eyes.

Spur heard the first shot as he cleared the last few trees, then heard more. Earlier McCoy had

146

noticed noise from the forest, but had assumed it was deer running, or some cows that had wandered off the pasture. He raced his horse toward the spot, waiting for another blast. None came.

Spur found the trampled brush—someone had walked through there quite recently. Running Bear, the Indian he'd just spoken with? He followed the trail until he saw another to his right, apparently headed in the same direction.

Two minutes later he saw a prostrate form. As he stopped beside it he recognized the face. Running Bear.

Spur dismounted and touched his shoulder. He was dead. Spur shook his head and hurried back onto the horse, raced through the woods toward Hanging Rocks. When he cleared the trees he hadd a brief glimpse of two figures on a cliff three miles from him. Spur could just make them out—two men on horseback, one tall and the other short. They disappeared over the cliff before he could study them further. He couldn't make out their faces, horses, clothing—nothing. A pair of Indian killers, a tall one and a short one, who'd just shot the peace loving Running Bear.

He turned his horse to follow the men but a cry from the woods halted him. The Navajo must have found Running Bear. Spur knew he wouldn't catch the men now; they were long gone. He turned for the forest and rode back to Running Bear's body.

Ten braves from the reservation, including Crooked Finger, surrounded their dead friend. Crooked Finger looked at Spur gravely, pointed to Running Bear, then to Spur. He pantomimed shooting a gun.

Spur shook his head.

The Indians muttered to each other. Apparently

none spoke English. Crooked Finger stared at Running Bear, then back at Spur. With excellent mimicry he *pulled* a gun from his invisible holster and handed it to Spur.

McCoy shook his head. "I don't understand."

Crooked Finger approached him carefully and motioned for Spur to dismount. He did so, and the Indian, staring into Spur's eyes, reached for his Colt.

Spur grabbed Crooked Finger's hand. When the man's expression didn't change Spur brushed it away, drew his gun and held it in both hands before him.

The Indian extended his hands. Spur didn't understand. Did he want his gun?

Crooked Finger pointed to the Colt, then to his nose. Gun, nose? Then Spur knew. He would do it if it'd made them believe he hadn't shot Running Bear. He gave the Navajo the Colt, half prepared for the man to use it on him, if only out of principle. Spur trusted him—partly.

Crooked Finger raised the gun's barrel to his nose, sniffed, smiled and handed it back to Spur, with some words to his friends. Together they lifted Running Bear's body and started for the reservation.

McCoy's gun had not been fired recently. The Indians knew he didn't kill Running Bear.

"Makkoi," Crooked Finger said, looking back at him.

"What?"

"Find," the Indian said thickly.

Spur nodded and watched the men leave, then frowned as he saddled up and rode home. At least he knew that the men who killed Running Bear were of different heights—a difference that showed even in the saddle. He wondered if they were the same ones who had massacred the whites.

He also knew that Indians were indeed being killed, so the Navajo hadn't been lying about that.

McCoy wished Running Bear eternal peace as he rode toward the cliff and Hanging Rocks.

FIFTEEN

"Hello, Mr. McCoy!" Margaret Bishop said as Spur entered Sheriff Hughes' office. She held a cloth-covered basket.

"Good afternoon, Miss Bishop, Mr. Hughes," Spur said, glancing at each of them in turn.

"Hi, McCoy." Vance Hughes sat behind his desk chewing on an unlit cigar.

"I'm just bringing Vance some of my freshly baked cinnamon rolls," Margaret said, placing the basket on Hughes' desk and flipping back the cloth.

Spur smelled their delicious scent before he saw the striped round pastries.

"They smell mighty fine to me!" Hughes said, putting down his cigar. "Thank you, Margaret. I'm sure I won't be able to wait until dinner."

"You promise me," Margaret said, and shook her short finger at him. Margaret Bishop wore a light brown dress, much cheerier than the one she'd worn when Spur had last seen her. The woman turned to him and sighed. "I guess you two have business, so I'll be running back home. Nice to see you again, Mr. McCoy."

"You two know each other?" the sheriff asked.

"Yes." Margaret smiled. "Why, if it wasn't for this man I'd be dead now."

"Mrs. Bishop!" Spur said. "That's not quite true."

"He rescued me from my runaway carriage yesterday." Margaret looked at Spur, her face radiant.

"I see," Hughes said, amused, and then glanced at Spur.

"I have to go. Goodbye, gentlemen."

The men said their farewells. As Margaret turned to walk to the door Spur spoke to the sheriff.

"I went out to the reservation today, talked with some Indians. One of them was killed just after I left. Running Bear, I think his name was."

He heard a gasp behind him and turned. Margaret stood in the doorway, motionless.

"Are you all right, Mrs. Bishop?" Spur asked.

"Yes, I'm fine." She turned to them. "Maybe I'm overtired, all this baking and housecleaning today." Margaret looked at Hughes. "Do you mind if I set myself for a spell?"

"Of course not," Hughes said, jumping up. "Use my chair."

"No, this is fine." Margaret settled into a straight backed chair next to the locked gun rack. "Please, don't let me disturb you, Mr. McCoy. I'm fine, really."

As Spur looked at her he knew she wasn't, but let it pass. He'd ask her later. McCoy turned back to Hughes. "As I was saying, the Indian I'd talked with was killed."

"By who?" Hughes asked.

"I don't know; just barely got a glance at them."

"There was more than one killer?"

152

"Looked that way."

Hughes smiled. "Are you sure it wasn't just some local trouble among their own?"

Spur shook his head. "No. I've got an idea that whoever killed Running Bear also killed the other Indians from Echo Creek."

Hughes was silent for a moment, then looked at Spur coldly. "So? What do we care? They're not under our protection. They're not U.S. citizens."

A sudden movement from Margaret made Spur turn to look at her. She sat, her arms resting on her thighs, bent over slightly, hands folded. She almost seemed to be praying.

"I also think there may be a link between the Navajo deaths and the ranch massacres," he said after turning back to the sheriff.

Hughes shook his head. "I don't understand. Why the hell would the two be related?"

"Just thought you should know."

"You said you went out to see the Navajos. Did you find anything? Did the men who killed the MacDonalds and the Goodnights confess?"

Spur looked sharply at the sheriff.

"All right, all right. You've got your theories and I've got mine."

"The Navajo didn't kill the ranchers," Spur said. He felt Margaret's gaze.

"No? Then would you mind telling me who did?" Hughes slid back into his chair.

Spur shrugged. "I don't know. But he's here in Hanging Rocks."

Hughes laughed. "Now you're saying we're killing our own."

"I saw them."

"Who?"

"The two men who killed Running Bear. They

153

had to be the ones."

"Did you follow them?"

Spur shook his head. "No. I got called away. Besides, they would have been back to Hanging Rocks before I could have caught up with them. They rode out fast."

"You keep me informed," Hughes said, and shook his head. "Goddamn. Next you'll be telling me—oh, beg your pardon, Mrs. Bishop. I'd forgotten you were there."

"It's quite all right, Sheriff." Margaret seemed to have composed herself. "I'll go now and have a rest at home."

"You do that," Hughes said, and looked at Spur. "Maybe you should see her home, to make sure she gets there all right. We can't have her swooning all over town!"

"Really, I'm fine—" Margaret began.

"Would you mind?" Spur asked.

The woman sighed. "It would be a pleasure. Good day, Vance," she said to the sheriff.

"Good afternoon." Hughes gave Spur a curious glance. "You take care of her."

"I will."

Spur walked beside the woman toward Oak Street.

"I—I feel so foolish about what happened to me," Margaret said, her cheeks burning as she spoke. "Sometimes I act like an old woman—or a child."

"No need to apologize." Spur remembered that she'd burst out as he mentioned the killed Indian. "Were you upset that another Navajo was killed?"

She looked at him in amazement, then quickly diverted her eyes. "Yes." Margaret's voice was neutral. "You're very bright, Mr. McCoy."

"It's my job."

Margaret sighed. "So much violence. Although I hate to say it, maybe it would be a good idea if the reservation could be moved. At least there wouldn't be these problems between the Navajo and the whites."

"That's the easy way out," Spur said. "Who could say that that wouldn't hurt the Indians, or just cause problems somewhere else? We can't solve a problem by pushing it aside," Spur said gently. "Begging your pardon, ma'am, but the way I see it, folks have to learn to get along with each other, no matter what god they pray to, whiskey they drink or what color their skins are."

"No need to apologize," Margaret said. "You're probably right—no, you *are* right." She sighed. "But you don't know the people who live in Hanging Rocks. You wouldn't believe the talk I've heard —oh hello, Emma!" she said to a middle-aged woman with a pinched face and gray hair, who waved on her way to the general store, three dirty children trailing after her. "What was I saying?"

"You were talking about what you've heard in town."

"That's right!" She shivered. "That's why I don't go out much these days, except for my weekly rides." Margaret suddenly turned from him, covered her face with a hand and stopped walking.

Startled by her sudden change of mood, Spur touched her shoulder. "Mrs. Bishop?" he asked.

"I'm sorry," she said between sobs. "I'm being such a fool." She wiped her eyes and wouldn't look at him. "Let's just walk on home."

They did so in silence. At the front door

155

Margaret turned to him. "I'm—forgive me for the way I've acted today. I've been so—tired lately."

She hadn't seemed tired when he'd walked into the sheriff's office, but her eyes seemed dead now. "Mrs. Bishop, I know it's none of my business, and you're not beholden to answer any of my questions. But what really upset you?"

Margaret looked at him, eyelashes smoothed into spikes by her tears. "You—you wouldn't understand."

"Try me."

She sniffed, paused, then nodded. "Would you come in for a cup of coffee?" Margaret opened the door.

Spur smiled. "Yes."

Margaret was pensive as they entered the parlor, eyes darting left and right, hands clasping and unclasping before her. She led him to the chairs. As they sat Margaret sighed. "It's so—frightfully difficult to discuss."

"You don't have to say a word if you don't want to." Spur wondered what was bothering her. Margaret might respect the Navajo as a group, but she seemed to broken up by the news of the man's death.

"I—I *knew* Running Bear." She looked away from him, out the window at the blue sky.

Something in the way she'd said *knew* triggered a signal in Spur's brain.

"You what?"

"You're probably wondering how I met an Indian man. I was out riding in the woods one day —and had an accident. Running Bear—helped me." She fidgeted in her chair.

"Okay," Spur said. She was lying.

"So naturally when you said that he—that

156

Running Bear had been killed—I was horrified! He wasn't some faceless Indian—he was a man I knew."

"I see. Why didn't you just say so?"

Margaret laughed hollowly. "You know what the people around here think of the Navajo. If they *guessed* that I had ever talked with one I'd be ridiculed."

"I find that hard to believe," Spur said. "But then I don't live here." He studied her. "There's something else, isn't there? Something you're not telling me?"

"No," Margaret said, her voice shaking.

"What was it?"

She looked at him sharply. "What was what?"

"The accident; the one that Running Bear helped you with?"

Her face melted and she cried shamelessly. "I'm sorry," she said. "There I go, apologizing again!"

She seemed too broken up. The way she'd told the story, Spur thought, she'd only seen him once. Or had she?

"I must look a sight," Margaret choked out. "If you want to go I wouldn't blame you."

"You look fine," Spur said in a soothing voice. "Did you see Running Bear again? Maybe out in the woods where you drive?"

"I did—yes, yes I did," Margaret looked at him in astonishment, her sobbing halted. "Mr. McCoy, you seem to know more about it than I do!"

"No," he said. "Just asking questions."

Margaret frowned. "Heaven help me, I can't. I just can't tell you!" she hissed.

"No one's forcing you."

"But I have to tell someone! Mr. McCoy, Running Bear was—was—" Her face wrinkled

157

with effort and her eyes flooded. "He was my—" Margaret looked at him squarely. "Do I have to spell it out for you?"

Spur knew. It all fit. He didn't alter his expression as he realized the truth. "I see." Running Bear had been Margaret Bishop's lover. Incredible. *Unbelievable!* No wonder she'd been concerned for his people and had reacted as she had at the news of his death.

"You probably think I'm some kind of beast, an unclean woman," Margaret said, grabbing her shoulders with crossed arms and looking at him, tears rolling down her face.

"No."

"Sure you do! I know what Vance or Emma or the rest of my friends would think if they even suspected. They'd probably spit at me in the street," she said bitterly.

"I doubt that."

Margaret turned to him. "Do you? I guess it doesn't matter now. He's dead. It's over. And Now I'm alone—again."

Spur sat in silence for a moment as Margaret rose and moved about the room as if entranced.

"Alone again," she said. "After my first husband died I said I'd never be involved with another man." Margaret glared at him. "I never should have broken that vow. Look what it's cost me!"

"And look what it gave you! What would you have lost, missed out on, if you hadn't broken that promise!" Spur asked, and looked out the window.

"I don't know. Maybe it would have been better—"

"Mrs. Bishop, who are those men?" he asked, interrupting her.

"Who? What men?" She wiped her eyes and went to the window.

Two men rode up to the Stanton House—one was tall, the other much shorter.

"Oh, that's Michael Stanton and Dave Colby."

"Which is which?" Spur asked as the men rode around the house.

"Michael Stanon is the taller one."

Spur frowned. "I think I know who killed Running Bear, and maybe the MacDonalds and the Goodnights," he said, peering out the window. The two men rode behind the house and disappeared, probably headed for stables.

"Who?" Margaret asked timidly.

They could be the same ones, Spur thought; same size, certainly. But the motive?

"Who?" Margaret's voice was harsher, demanding. "Tell me who killed Running Bear!"

"I'm not sure—yet. Margaret, do you mind if I watch out your window again?"

"You—you called me Margaret," she said, her eyes lighting in wonder.

"I'm sorry. I wasn't thinking."

"No, that's fine. After what you know about me—" She shook her head. "Formalities are sort of ridiculous."

"Then call me Spur. I hope you don't mind if I use your window again."

"No, not at all. I'll feel safer—I mean, I won't feel so alone, now that Running Bear's . . . gone."

Margaret turned and walked from him. Spur settled into the chair, still staring at the Stanton house. It was almost implausible that the man who killed the ranchers and Running Bear had just ridden to the house across the street. Still, Spur had a feeling.

"Make yourself comfortable," Margaret said. "I'll fix some coffee and bring you a cinnamon roll."

"That sounds wonderful." Spur settled in before the window as Margaret walked off, blocking out an image of the powerful Indian and helpless woman coupling among the pines and cottonwoods.

SIXTEEN

Spur drained another cup of coffee. Nothing had changed at the Stanton House, save for the lights which had glowed on at dusk. At eleven most of the windows were dark except one section about twenty feet long.

He slid the window open. A breeze swept into Margaret Bishop's parlor, rustling the curtains and bringing the bittersweet scent of mesquite smoke.

Nothing. No change. No one had left or entered the house since he'd taken up his position. Spur felt his bladder scream and so slipped from the parlor, through the hall and out the back door, then to the outhouse.

Done with his business, Spur went back in the house to the parlor, where he lifted his empty cup automatically, stared into it, then set it down on the table beside him. Was it worth staying up all night? Would he see anything?

"How's it going?" Margaret asked as she walked into the parlor, carrying a steaming coffee pot.

"Fine." He held out his cup.

"Any luck?" Her face was hopeful.

Spur shook his head. "Not so far."

"You look tired."

"No, just bored."

Margaret filled his cup and handed it to him. "I'll be reading in my bedroom. I can't sleep tonight; not with what's happened."

Spur nodded. "Sure."

"Are you planning on spending the night?"

He looked at her in surprise. "Beg your pardon?"

Margaret's face reddened. "I'm sorry; I meant, do you think you'll watch the house till morning?"

Spur smiled. "Don't know for sure. It depends on how tired I get."

"If you do leave before dawn, come in and let me know. I'll probably be awake." She looked at him curiously. "Would you?"

"Sure."

"Thank you. Good luck, Spur."

"Enjoy your book."

Fifteen minutes later Spur set down his dry coffee cup and rose. He was going home. Nothing would happen tonight. Spur headed for the front door, then remembered the promise he'd made to Margaret. He went to the bedroom at the rear of the house and, seeing a light on under the half-closed door, raised his hand to knock.

Then he heard her—the low pants, sharp cries, a series of heartfelt *ohs*. Must be some book, he thought, standing before the door motionless, listening.

"Oh Spur, Spur!" Margaret said.

Did she know he was there? She couldn't. Spur had to see what she was doing. He pushed the door gently inward and peered around it.

Margaret was lying on the bed, legs spread, wearing a nearly transparent black nightgown. Her right hand moved quickly between her legs, and the other caressed her breasts, pinching her firm nipples under the shiny cloth.

Her eyes closed as she stimulated herself.

"Spur!" she called out again, jerking her head back and forth, her legs crossing and then uncrossing alternately as she fingered her clitoris.

He couldn't take much more of this. Spur felt the pressure at his crotch.

"Spur, help me!" she wailed.

Her voice made his penis throb with its wild ululation. Spur watched her tongue caress her lips, her hips grind and bump on the bed, her hand a blur as she rubbed herself to a climax.

She shook, her upper lip tight as her body flushed and she let out another howl. The bed squeaked and a few feathers shot out from the mattress.

Spur rubbed himself absentmindedly. If she was asleep, he didn't dare interfere. If she was begging him to pleasure her, he couldn't refuse.

Which was it?

She opened her eyes and stared straight at him. She wasn't sleeping. Margaret was wide awake and aroused. "Spur. Take me now!"

"What?" he said, startled by the sudden change.

"If you don't I'll never sleep with another man! I have to have new memories to block out the old ones! Running Bear's gone; I'll always love him, but love for a dead man doesn't warm the bed. If you have any respect for Running Bear," she said as she slipped off the nightgown, revealing her alabaster skin and flawless body: full hips, tiny waist, and bouncing breasts, "stop standing there and do what you want to do!"

Spur didn't hesitate. He reached down to pull off his boots.

"No time for that, damn you!" Margaret said, and shoved three fingers up herself. "Just pull it out and stick it in there!" She licked the fingers. "Or here! But stick it somewhere so I don't taste Running Bear's organ sliding between my lips or feel his thrusts between my legs. Sweet Jesus, Spur; treat me like the woman I am and *use me!*"

Spur ripped his fly open, pushed down his pants and short underdrawers, and released his penis. Before it could swing up Margaret had pounced to the floor, cat-like, then knelt before him and slurped his erection into her mouth.

Her head bobbed fiercely, lips suctioning around the shaft and head while she gently squeezed his scrotum and testicles. Margaret took him as if she thought she'd never suck again.

"Jeezus!" Spur said. "Goddamn, Margaret! Yeah! Show me what you can do!"

She pulled off him, "Fuck my mouth," she said lustily, staring up hungrily at him, then leaned her head back and parted her lips.

Spur did as she ordered, gripping her head and pushing into the warm mouth and constricting throat. Margaret took his entire length like no woman ever had, and Spur looked at her in amazement and near agony as she buried her nose in his pubic hair while staring up at him.

The woman swallowed and Spur felt his groin threaten to erupt. He pulled out and heard her gasp before plunging back home.

After a few strokes Spur sighed and withdrew from her mouth completely.

"Why'd you stop?" Margaret demanded, licking her lips.

"You said you wanted it everywhere."

"I never said—well, maybe I did." Margaret

smiled, her brows lowered. "Yes. Stick me, Spur."
She started to move to the bed, but McCoy
grabbed her arm roughly.

"No. On the floor." He pointed to the sheepskin
rugs lying behind her.

Margaret's eyes gleamed as she fell back onto
the lush fur, then giggled as Spur parted her legs.

Spur stared down at the flash of pink in her red-
haired bush. It seemed to draw him in almost mag-
ically. McCoy knelt, cupped her bottom and lifted
her vagina to his mouth. He lapped at it hungrily.

Margaret gasped as he ate her. "Yes! That's
wonderful. Bite me!"

Spur licked and teethed her sensitive areas,
sending Margaret into an orgasm. As she lay pant-
ing he stretched over her and rammed into her wet
hole.

"Do it to me!" Margaret cried, her eyes aflame
—haunting, intense points of light. "You're—
you're so big! Bigger than Running Bear! Ahh!"
She reached down and gripped his shaft and balls,
using them as a handle to pull him into her.

Spur pumped in amazement as Margaret's hIps
raised to meet his. He didn't remember ever
meeting a woman who enjoyed sex as much as
Margaret Bishop. Where was the shy, demure
creature he'd known earlier? This woman was one
of the most uninhibited he'd ever met.

"Ram me harder, Spur!" she said. "Fuck Running Bear out of me. Do it, love!"

That kind of talk did what it was supposed to.
Spur's midsection exploded, followed by a mind
shattering, bone jarring orgasm. His hips pumped
involuntarily, slamming their bodies together as
multi-colored streaks of light passed his eyes.

Margaret clung to him, his climax sparking her

own. She moaned, squeezed him, shook and finally lay still as he panted in her ear, holding her shoulders, his member pulsing deep inside.

Spur's brain seemed full of mist as they held each other, and Margaret's higher, faster breaths rushed past his face. She laughed quietly.

"What's so funny?"

"You. I didn't know if you were going to take me up on my offer or not."

"You weren't sleeping while I was watching you, were you?"

She shook her head. "No. I had been reading. When I heard the hall floorboard squeak I put away the book and started rubbing myself, hoping you'd take the hint." She turned serious. "I'm not saying that I just wanted to get you in bed, Spur. It's not like that. Although you're an attractive man. I meant what I said about Running Bear— it'll be hard to forget him."

"Then don't," Spur said. "Not if he meant that much to you. But just because we remember the past doesn't mean we can't go on with the future."

"I'll try to remember that."

They kissed and Margaret pushed him off her. "Your shirt buttons are hurting me," she said.

"Sorry. You told me not to undress."

Margaret chuckled. "That's right; I'd forgotten."

"You know, Margaret, you sure had me fooled. I thought you were so prim and proper you wouldn't think of laying with a man unless he was your husband."

She laughed. "That's what I want people to think. But I'm no different from the rest of the women in Hanging Rocks, or anywhere. Half of the wives in this town have been unfaithful to their husbands at least once. I can practically guarantee it."

"Why?"

She sighed. "Wives get bored with their husbands and vice versa. Everybody has some fun now and then; it's just that nobody talks about it, except among themselves, like we're talking."

"I see."

She sat up. "I suppose you should be watching the Stanton house, right?"

He shrugged. "I'd decided to go back to my hotel room."

"But you *should* watch the place." She glanced at the clock. "Eleven-thirty. Lots of things happen over there around this time of night."

"What kind of things?" Spur asked as he rose from the rug and pushed himself back into his fly, then buttoned it up.

"People coming and going a lot. He's seemed to have a great deal of late night company."

"At this hour? Women?"

"No, all men. You can see the house from the window." She pointed to it.

Spur looked outside. Two men walked to the Stanton house's porch and walked inside without bothering to knock. He turned back to Margaret.

"Am I right?" she asked.

He nodded. "What the hell's going on over there?"

"I don't know. It's been happening for a few weeks now. I can't sleep a lot—thinking of Running Bear, wanting him beside me—so I'd sit at the window and stare at the moon and stars. I also saw the activity at Mr. Stanton's home." She looked down. "I realize it's important for you to watch his home, but if you'd like to make some more memories with me I'd be more than willing. Just say the word."

Spur looked at the attractive, naked woman, her hair mussed, eyes sleepy but sex-infused. "I should watch it," he said, moving reluctantly to the bedroom door.

Margaret sighed. "Okay. But you know where to find me if you want some more." She laid on the bed and yawned, then reached over to turn down the kerosene lamp on a bedside table. "Good night, Spur. And thank you."

"My pleasure."

A half hour later twelve men had entered Stanton's house while Spur watched. All remained inside. The flame lit windows were completely draped, ruling out any possibility of watching. Spur could move to the house quietly and listen in, but there were no plants or cover near the windows —he'd be in plain sight of anyone who happened by.

He frowned and waited.

An hour later the men had left. Spur watched as the windows went dark. A light in an upstairs room glowed for a few moments, then died. Stanton must have gone to bed. He waited another hour, staring at the house, then left the parlor and walked out the back door. Spur circled around Margaret's house and stood in its shadow, contemplating the two story structure across the street, now dark and apparently quiet.

He had the urge to go inside, to search for evidence which would link Stanton with the ranchers' murders, but didn't know what he could find that would support his feelings.

Spur's legs suddenly seemed to move of their

own accord as he casually walked across the street and then beside the house. Glancing around to see if anyone was watching, Spur slipped behind Stanton's mansion and looked for the back door.

SEVENTEEN

No one had mentioned it. Eagle Feather ran a stained finger over his smooth ribs on the dull gray blanket that lay stretched over him as he stared up. He felt the earth's chill through the meager bedding, and his teeth threatened to chatter.

After Running Bear's body was given to the gods, things in the camp went along as before. Still, the chief sensed the village's loss—two of the strongest men were gone.

None came to Eagle Feather, or looked at him when he went to relieve himself in the bushes, their eyes saying *You killed him!* None of his people had accused him of murdering Rainbow Dream, though everyone knew he had.

He was chief. Chiefs were allowed to break the laws, if for the good of the tribe.

Eagle Feather sighed as the image flashed vividly into his mind—Rainbow Dream's face as he died. The old magics were still powerful, the chief thought. The spells still worked. Rainbow Dream had fallen victim to them.

He clearly remembered plunging the knife into the man's chest, but this did not shake his faith in magic. The spell had already killed him; the knife

171

was just a formality.

He remembered how Singing Jay had cried when she saw him at her hogan. She had known that her man was dead. Eagle Feather sniffed and rolled onto his side painfully, the wound on his chest throbbing. His usually quick, shallow breath increased in rate at the slight effort.

Why didn't he just die? Maybe he should have let Rainbow Dream kill him. It would have been comforting to slip into the blackness of death, no longer needing to worry for his people and allow Rainbow Dream to ruin them when he was gone.

"No," he said aloud. Better if they could have killed each other. But it was too late now.

Eagle Feather hoped Makkoi—the strange white man who had told them of Running Bear's death— would find the man who killed the Navajo. The forest and even open areas around the reservation were so dangerous that he'd had to forbid all movement off their own lands. Earlier he'd allowed hunting parties to ride to richer areas, risking the white man's wrath, but no more.

Eagle Feather would live until he saw his people stop dying. The old man's eyes flickered, closed, opened and sank down again. If he wasn't afraid to die, the chief asked himself, why was he frightened of sleep? He'd heard that sleep was a death that ended each morning, and the thought comforted him.

Chief Eagle Feather relaxed into the darkness.

They'd finally stopped—Caroline sighed as she realized the noise downstairs had ceased. Her father's rantings—still as unintelligible as ever— had halted, and in their place was uncustomary silence.

She sighed loudly and fussed with the down comforter. Caroline expected to melt into the still-ness but found she couldn't. She heard a coyote's wailing somewhere in the desert outside and the wind thrashing nearby pines. As much as she dis-liked her father's screaming, it seemed friendlier than the desert's night sounds.

Though Hanging Rocks was a pleasant enough place to live, with substantial buildings, an opera house and a good sized trade, the wilderness dwelled not far beyond its limits. Caroline thought of that as she lay waiting for sleep.

The girl remembered the ride from Phoenix, how empty land stretched in every direction as far as she could see—some incredibly beautiful, some stark and ugly. The endless viewes, valleys stretching out into other valleys, mountains loom-ing and the ragged desert floor flecked with cactus trees—the images boiled up in her mind. Hanging Rock' isolation in the immense Arizona Territory sent a chill through her.

An hour later, she hadn't slept. Caroline had almost decided to rise and light the lamp when she heard a noise downstairs.

Her father? No, he'd gone to bed. She was sure of it. It seemed to come from the back of the house. Caroline slipped from the bed, put on a robe and walked down the stairs to the rear of the house, tip-toeing most of the way, the polished wood floors clinging to her feet.

Caroline heard no more sounds. She walked to the back door, found it closed, and looked through the kitchen and pantry. Nothing out of the ordinary. Maybe she'd imagined it.

Caroline turned and nearly screamed when she saw a man standing in the doorway, lit by the

moonlight streaming in through the kitchen
window.

"Dave!" she said.

"Hi, Caroline." Colby stood fully dressed,
looking at her, leaning against the doorframe.

"What are you doing down here? You gave me a
fright!"

"Getting something to eat. I'm starved."

Caroline shook her head as she walked to the
door. "I thought someone might have broken in."

"No. Only me." He blocked the door with his
arms. "You know, Caroline, your father's asleep.
Do you feel like—"

"Now?" she asked.

"Sure, why not? It's night, and he's not likely to
walk in on us."

"No," she said firmly. Dave irritated her.

"Okay, okay; just asking." He moved and
allowed her to pass. "But why not?"

"It's the middle of the night!" she said. "I'm
sleepy and—and—oh, I don't know, Dave! I just
don't feel like it. I'm sorry."

"It's the middle of the morning, but okay."

"Try not to make too much noise."

He smiled. "Sure."

"And don't you steal another bottle of cherries!"
she warned him. "Cook will kill you if she's
missing another one."

"I won't."

Caroline knew he would anyway. "Never mind.
I'm going back to bed and hopefully to sleep." She
looked at him suddenly. "What are you doing up
this late?"

"I told you—I was hungry."

"Father had another meeting, didn't he?"

Colby shook his head. "Can't talk about it." He

walked to the pantry. "See you in the morning. I'm hungry."

Caroline sighed and hurried back to her room, sure that she could sleep now. She yawned as she breezed into her bedroom, slipped off the robe, threw it onto the bed and laid inside her warm covers.

She slept.

Spur turned the knob at the rear of the Stanton home. The door opened as he pulled it away from the house. McCoy slid inside, closed it and turned to look around him.

He was in the kitchen, and a door that might lead to a pantry lay to his immediate left. Spur turned to look into it—a thin shaft of light penetrated the darkness. He saw bottles and shelves, with sacks of flour, beans and other staples lying on the floor.

As he started out of the kitchen into the rest of the home he heard footsteps growing louder. Spur ducked into the pantry, past two double sided rows of shelves of preserves. He went behind the third, crouched in the shadows, and waited.

The person moved into the pantry. Spur pulled an empty flour sack from the corner and threw it over him as he squatted.

"No. That's all the food you need tonight, Colby," a female voice said. The footsteps moved off.

When the man had left Spur removed the sack and stood. Something shining in the corner, partially concealed by the bag he'd thrown onto it, caught his attention. It looked like gold.

Spur reached down and felt material, then braid. He pulled out a colonel's shirt, but one the likes of which he'd never seen. It was a uniform of an army unknown to Spur. He found two boxes in the space where two walls of shelves abutted, nearly touching. The boxes had obviously been placed there with great difficulty, probably by moving the shelves of preserves, and they had been deliberately hidden.

Why?

Spur shrugged and, replacing the uniform and the sack that had concealed it, quickly checked the rest of the pantry. He found more uniforms, Winchester rifles and ammunition, all carefully secreted so that no one could find them unless looking for them.

Spur could only guess that Stanton was organizing a group of fighting men—either that or selling the goods. But the uniforms seemed to suggest a private army.

Stanton could be organizing to fight the Navajo. He was probably doing so now; the small controntations which were leaving more and more of the Navajo dead were suspicious.

There was only one way Spur could see it— Stanton had killed Running Bear, the ten Navajo and the ranching families. He planned to wipe the Indians out, spread public dissent, and had killed the MacDonalds and Goodnights to whip up sentiment against the Navajo. If Spur was right, Stanton must be completely consumed by his desire to destroy the Navajo nation. McCoy wanted to know why.

The men who had come to the house earlier that night might be members of Stanton's army. He was playing it safe—wasn't taking any chances. He obviously was organizing an aboveboard, legal militia. Stanton was building a private army.

Spur had seen enough. He left the pantry and

moved quietly back to the kitchen, then slipped out the back entrance and closed the door. The Secret Service man walked to Oak Street and moved along it to Broad and the Cicily Hotel. Maybe he could catch a few hours of sleep before watching the Stanton place again.

He thought wistfully of Margaret and her warm bed, but knew he would get precious little sleep there. As it was he hoped he'd have time to close his eyes before sunrise.

EIGHTEEN

Michael Stanton sat on the bed in the darkened room, waiting for dawn. He didn't want to sleep. That was for weaklings who couldn't think after sundown.

The meeting had gone well that night, Stanton thought, grinning as he remembered his delight at the number of men who'd attended—eighteen. The army was growing quickly. More of the good men of Hanging Rocks were waking to the dangers of the vicious Navajos. He smiled. They'll be rid of the Indians yet.

Then Stanton punched his bed. He'd been thinking that for so long, all these months. Finally, a month ago, he'd moved from the planning stages to action, and had killed some Navajo with Colby and a few men. They followed up that strike with a raid on the ranchers—not only because that goddamned Doug MacDonald had tried to cheat him out of ten dollars at the faro table in the Placer Saloon—may his soul rot in *hell*, Stanton thought —but also because the ranchers' closeness to the reservation might lead people to think that the Navajos had killed them. So they'd stuffed their feet into moccasins, rode there, killed them, walked around in the moccasins and threw Indian artifacts around that he'd picked up over the years, then rode out.

Stanton smiled as he remembered how he, Colby and two other trusted men had ridden to the Mac-Donalds ranch in midmorning. They'd picked off the hands at long range and then tracked down Gertrude MacDonald and her children and gunned them down. He'd always hated that family anyway, with their squealing children and that ugly Gertrude.

Doug MacDonald didn't have time to get a rifle before Stanton had ridden up to him.

"You!" MacDonald had said, blubbering like an idiot. "You—killed them! You killed them all!"

"Quit crying," Stanton had said. "You're joining them soon. I figured you wouldn't want to be away from them."

"No! You wouldn't shoot me. I'm unarmed!" The man threw his beefy hands up into the air.

"Bad planning on your part," Stanton had said, then plowed a bullet into his gut.

MacDonald screamed as blood flowed from the wound. His eyes slid up and he dropped to the ground.

Stanton had kicked the downed man. "Goddamn you, MacDonald!" Stanton shouted. "Why the hell did you try to steal my hard earned money yesterday at the Placer?"

Doug's eyes opened and he looked up at Stanton in disblief. "Jesus Christ!" he said, his voice gurgling. "You gut-shot me!"

"Yeah," Stanton said quickly, smiling. "Painful as hell, I'll bet. Feels like someone poured acid on you and it's eating you away." He'd grinned. "You

180

aren't smiling now, MacDonald; not like you were when you tried to cheat me at faro!''

''I never tried—''

''Bullshit!''

''I swear,'' MacDonald said. His face had gone white, his pupils pinpoints of concentrated fear. MacDonald shook his head and blubbered.

Stanton laughed. ''Hey Colby; come over here and look at this!'' he called.

His second appeared and stared down at MacDonald from his mount. ''He ain't dead yet?''

''No. I'm just watching how ridiculous he looks. Jesus Christ!'' he said, watching as a circular stain spread out from the man's crotch. ''He's pissed his pants!'' Stanton dropped to his feet and drove a foot into the man's groin.

Doug MacDonald's midsection spasmed as he fainted. Stanton stared down at him hopefully, hearing his other two men riding up.

''Is he dead?'' Colby asked.

MacDonald's chest continued to heave. Stanton smiled. ''Not yet. Wake up, MacDonald!''

Colby stepped from his mount, filled a bucket at the trough nearby, and handed it to Stanton.

''Thanks!'' he said with a low laugh. ''MacDonald!''

No response. The man lay prone, eyes closed, his body jerking as it oozed life.

Snarling, Stanton tipped the bucket over MacDonald's face, sending the water flying. It slapped against its target, the force of the impact pushing out his cheeks and rippling the skin in his neck. MacDonald sputtered but didn't open his eyes.

The man's breath had turned shallow, and

181

Stanton frowned. "Goddamn you, wake up! I'm not going to let you die yet, you stealing mother-fucker!"

Colby was silent as Stanton glared down at the man, eyes wide, lips slick, gasping. He looked around him and spotted a saw nearby, then looked at Colby.

"Haul his pants down," Stanton said coldly.

"Do what?"

"Pull his pants down." He flexed the saw meaningfully.

Colby smiled and bent over the prostrate man. He struggled and soon had the man's groin bare in the hot sun.

Stanton stood over the man, shook the saw, and kicked him once. MacDonald moved, roused, his eyes open, then focused on Stanton, infused with fear.

"I always said you didn't have any balls," Stanton said, as he lowered the saw and placed the tip at the man's crotch.

"Christ!" MacDonald gurgled.

Stanton sliced through the soft skin, severing the man's genitals. Blood spurted out in fountains, shining in the sun, as MacDonald fainted.

Stanton threw down the saw and looked back at Colby. "Leave him. He'll be dead in three minutes. Let's get the hell out of here!"

Colby stared at the man, seemingly in shock.

"Didn't you hear me? Move it!"

Colby snapped out of his trance and they rode off.

"That showed that asshole," Stanton said. He directed the other men to ride on ahead so that they wouldn't all arrive in town together.

"Goddamn, Mr. Stanton!" Colby said, wide-eyed, as they rode. "When you get your revenge you don't do it halfway!"

"Hell no!" His face was grim. "If a man's going to do something there's no reason to do it halfway. You either do it or you don't."

"Yeah, but sawing off his balls and dick?" Colby asked in amazement.

Stanton shrugged. "It'll make folks think he was killed by the Indians. They do things like that."

Colby looked at Stanton with what seemed to be near reverence, and Stanton hadn't liked it. "Get that shit-eating grin off your face," he said, and rode on ahead.

Back in town, they had a drink to celebrate, Stanton remembered fondly. He glanced at the window, which showed the sky to be unchanged black. How long until morning? He was in the mood to do some hunting. He was sure he'd be lucky and find Navajos off the reservation. If not, he might just ride onto their land and pick a few off —but he was well aware of the dangers.

Stanton remembered Colby's face that morning, the admiration that had shone there. What the hell. He'd invite the kid along too. Might as well, even though he'd nearly fucked up the last time. Colby needed the practice.

He rose and peered out the window. To the east he saw the slightest lightening of the black sky, as if someone had lifted the curtains in that direction. First light. Stanton dressed and went to Colby's room, knocked and then walked in.

"Colby!" he said, shaking the man who lay bare chested, face up on the bed.

He groaned. "What?"

"Goddamn it, Colby! You'll probably snore through your own murder. Wake up! We've got some hunting to do."

Colby lay still for a moment, then opened his eyes. "You said the right thing." He yawned wider, his throat producing a strange high noise. "Jesus Christ," he said, rubbing his head. "I feel like I was horsekicked."

'You drink too much. I'll make some coffee. Be dressed and in the kitchen in five minutes. Got that? Five." He held out a hand, fingers spread. "Unless you don't want to come with me. I'm giving you another chance after you nearly lost us that last Indian."

Colby's eyes widened and he rubbed the grit from them. "Okay, okay." He sat up and slid his feet to the floor. "Christ, it's cold."

"Yeah. Hurry up." Stanton left the man and went to the kitchen to make the coffee. After thinking all night, he could use it. He fixed his mind on the Navajos as he smelled the bitter scent from the pot and imagined the coming hunt.

NINETEEN

"We go now!" the tallest of the three Navajo men said as they squatted a thousand feet from their camp. "Before it is light."

The youngest, not quite seventeen, glanced at the east fearfully. "Morning has begun!" Fear gripped him, churned in his stomach. So many of their people had died.

"It doesn't matter," the eldest said. "We go. You know our tribe's hunting lands are nearly dead —we've killed all the animals because we haven't moved. The orchards are dying little by little, and our corn grows scraggly and the swellings don't come. We need the meat. That is plain. And it is worth the risks."

"But Chief Eagle Feather said—" the youngest began.

"It does not matter," the third man muttered. "We go. Do you go with us?"

The youngest glanced at his friends, trying to kill the chill of fear. He nodded.

They rose and launched themselves into a slow run, one they could maintain for hours, day or night. They each carried a bow and three arrows, and wore leather bowguards and breech cloths.

185

They struck out off Echo Creek Reservation onto the land of the round eyes who had treated them so cruelly. As they ran, the tall young brave moved with triumph at having disobeyed the round eye's rules.

They would get meat, the youngest one hoped. Sheep, or deer, and they would have another filling meal like they had had in the days before this strange, sad life.

He chanted a song to the gods which Chief Eagle Feather had once told him would ensure their favor in their battle or hunting. He sang to the animals, calling to them, singing his songs of hunger and need to the four quarters, then above and below in the sacred manner, again repeating the words.

He had done all he could. Now they had to move cautiously on white man's land, have a successful hunt, and not add their own deaths to the tribe's miseries.

As they ran he felt sweat spring out of his body, and the air chilled him.

Spur woke up as dawn paled the sky. He splashed water on his face at the basin, wiped on the fairly clean towel and shook his head. McCoy wrapped the gunbelt across his hips, tied down his holster; pocketed extra ammo and carried his Winchester from his hotel room into the cool morning air. Hanging Rocks woke as he slid the rifle into its boot on the saddle, then stepped up into it.

He rode to a spot five hundred yards from Stanton's home, in a place where he could watch the hitching post behind the house. Spur saw three horses in the stables.

He waited. Sometime Stanton would ride out to try to kill some more Navajo. Maybe not this morning, or tomorrow, but sometime. Spur had to make the effort to catch him doing it.

McCoy dismounted and tied up the horse as he relaxed beneath a stand of pines. The horse lifted its head and its eyes glazed over the sparse light before returning to normal. He browsed on the grass.

It seemed to have sensed evil. He'd seen horses do similar things many times. It was amazing how alien they were to him and all humans, Spur thought, yet how friendly and depending some could be.

He sighed and sat beneath the tree, leaned against its trunk, and watched the Stanton house. Maybe he'd be lucky.

A half hour later, Spur was startled to see the back door bang open and two men walk out of it—the same two men he'd seen ride in last night. He could only guess they were Stanton and—what was the name Margaret had said? Colby?

Spur mounted up, checked his weapons, and watched the men. They slid into their saddles and rode leisurely up Oak Street toward Broad.

Spur gently nudged his stallion forward, and the horse didn't balk. He moved down Oak two blocks from the men, then continued on across Broad and went north. To Echo Creek?

He followed them through town, dropping further back as they left it behind. Spur also moved off the trail, gaining some additional cover with the trees. Fortunately the land was fairly flat so he could keep the pair in sight while maintaining his distance.

As he rode he thought about the men—what had led Stanton to do all this—if indeed he had done it? And what kind of man was this Colby, who would follow him?

The pair wandered from the trail, poking slowly through the now thicker stands of trees. They were nearing the forest where Running Bear had been killed.

Spur dodged over again to coordinate with their movements and was surprised with the men reined in their mounts after they'd entered the woods. He followed suit and dismounted, slid out his rifle and tied his horse out of sight from the man's location.

Spur moved as silently as he could through the woods, circling around the men. Then he stopped and listened—there were sounds of a small party of men in the distance—two or three, Spur thought. He strained his ear and eyes—then saw three Indians about five hundred yards away, moving toward Stanton and Colby, who rode quickly back off the trail and waited.

As the Indians approached Spur knew what would happen—Stanton and Colby would ambush them.

When the group of hunters—Spur figured that's what they were—were still a hundred feet from the men, McCoy decided to speed things up.

"Don't do it, Stanton!" he yelled.

The Indians scattered as Stanton whirled and fired at Spur. The agent had already slammed down on the ground, fired over Stanton's head and rolled on his shoulder behind a pile of ancient boulders. Spur rose to his knees and blasted again, ducking below the rocks, dodging the returned fire.

Arrows sped through the air somewhere near him, and Spur turned to see an Indian look at him, apparently recognized McCoy, and lower his bow.

Good to have friends, Spur thought as he dove from the rocks to a three-foot thick tree. Spur shot over Stanton's head, who stood behind a tree, and Colby who was flattened on the ground.

Colby popped into view to take a shot. Spur fired, then again, thinking he'd missed. He heard a cry, then another, and Colby's rifle dropped from his hands. The man lay motionless on the ground, face down, bloodstains in the center of his shirt.

Probably dead, Spur decided. Stanton turned to look at the corpse, showing himself from behind the trunk. Spur fired but Stanton jolted and the slug sailed past him harmlessly.

Spur cursed as the man bolted to the right, heading for his horse, McCoy figured. He swung from behind the trunk and plowed a bullet into Stanton's right shoulder. The man screamed but kept running, past his horse, into a thick part of the woods that spread out before him.

McCoy cursed as he ran after Stanton. Just as he entered an incredibly lush area of forest, where trailing vines and bushes totally obscured the ground and ghostly morning mist filtered through the trees, he heard a sharp cry and then nothing.

Spur ran toward the sound but didn't see Stanton, probably because of the mist, he decided. Before he knew what had happened his feet touched air and he slid down a cliff. He clutched the Winchester to his chest as the earth burned his body, tore his clothing. McCoy bounced and tumbled down toward the unknown.

TWENTY

Spur groaned as he slid down the cliff on his butt, crashing through small bushes and dodging trees and rocks by throwing his weight to his right or left.

As the bushes slapped past him and trees rushed dizzingly close then disappeared, Spur heard crashing sounds below him down the cliff. Stanton must not have seen the valley's edge in the mist either. McCoy figured he'd fallen down a river-created valley.

Spur held his rifle with one hand and grabbed a small tree as he slid down. His fingers locked around the trunk but it bent under his pull and slipped out between his fingers.

McCoy tried again, grabbing a four-inch thick branch hanging above him from a pine. It held. He jumped up and planted his feet on the ground, motionless. Spur was bruised but nothing felt broken.

He heard a splash before him but the mist was thicker down there. Stanton must have landed in the creek. He heard more splashing sounds and rushed to them, expecting fire at any minute from Stanton. None came.

Spur's feet kicked something cold and shiny—he bent and picked it up. A Colt. Stanton had lost his weapon. He shoved it into his boot and then fired a warning shot into the air.

"Stanton!" he called, searching the mist as he moved forward. A tumble of rocks to his right made him turn in that direction. The mist was slowly dispersing, and he saw trees and the sparkle of the river—and Stanton crouching by a boulder, touching his bleeding right shoulder.

Spur went to the man.

"What the fuck do you want?"

"You were going to kill those three Navajo," Spur said.

"So? What the fuck concern is it of yours? Who the hell are you, anyway? You killed Colby, goddamn you!" His eyes flashed.

"I'm a U.S. government agent investigating the deaths of the MacDonalds and the Goodnights. You know anything about them?"

Stanton grimaced as he rubbed his shoulder. "Never heard of them."

"You're under federal arrest for their deaths," Spur said.

Stanton laughed. "Like hell I am!"

"You also killed Running Bear and several other Navajo. Do you deny it?"

"Hell no. Jesus Christ, where's my Colt? My rifle? Damn that cliff!"

"Come on, Stanton, it's over. Just walk quietly with me back to the horses. I'd rather see you stand before a judge and hang rather than gunning you down here and now. But don't think I wouldn't."

"You're scarin' me, boy! Scarin' me bad! I've got friends—I'm wealthy. You don't know who I am."

Stanton's face was lit by madness. "You haven't got a thing on me. I'm not going to—" Stanton's gaze locked onto something five feet from him on the ground.

Spur looked and saw the man's rifle.

"Don't think about going for it," he said. "You'll be dead before your fingers touch it."

"Damn you!" he said. "Fuck you!" Stanton pushed his body along the ground toward the rifle.

Spur blasted another slug into the man's shoulder, sending up a howl of pain from the big man.

"I'm warning you. You want another one through the heart, Stanton?" Spur asked, standing over him.

"Shit!" he said.

Spur heard men approaching on all sides. The Navajo, he figured. He wasn't surprised—word must have gone round that the man who was killing Indians was there—or perhaps they had simply heard the shooting.

"Piss on you!" Stanton said, then his eyes darted around him. "The goddamned injuns are on the warpath!" he said, his face streaked with color as he bled from both shoulders. "Do something! Let me get my rifle and help defend us!"

The Indians appeared, on all sides—there must have been thirty or more. They circled the two white men. Spur searched for a familiar face—and saw Crooked Finger, apparently leading the party. The Indian looked at Spur, smiled and called his men to halt.

Crooked Finger looked at Spur, pointed at Stanton, then drew back his bow.

"No," Spur said. "He is mine."

"Makkoi," he said. "Ours."

193

"Goddamn both of you!" Stanton screamed, his voice wheezing. "I'm not yours to give or take!"

"Shut up, Stanton; it's over. You're not going anywhere. You're under arrest for murder."

One of the Indians kicked Stanton and pushed him down onto the dirt.

"Keep your filthy hands offa me, goddamned redman!" he screamed.

Spur turned back to Crooked Finger. He pointed to Stanton, then to his chest. "Mine," he repeated.

Crooked Finger frowned as he stepped from the ring of Indians that kept Stanton and Spur penned in.

"Jesus Christ!" the white man said. "Don't you know what these Indians will do? They're savages. They'll torture us and—"

"Stanton, do you admit you killed the MacDonalds and the Goodnights?"

"Hell yes!" he said. "Just get these fuckin' Indians away from me!"

Crooked Finger pointed to Stanton, then made a sign to hold. Spur shook his head.

"*No.* He's my prisoner. For the government."

Crooked Finger frowned. "*Ejercito?*" he said.

"Yes, the army," Spur said, knowing it was the closest word the Indian probably had for government.

Crooked Finger looked at Spur, thinking, then shook his head.

"Goddamn you!" Stanton said. He pushed himself off the ground and lunged for his rifle.

Two dozen bows flew into action. Arrows drove into Stanton's body—through his chest, arms, back; one pierced an eye. The man screamed as his body, bristling with arrows, slumped to the ground. He lay still, oozing blood from thirty places.

Spur approached the man cautiously after the Indians had stopped shooting. Dead? Stanton's hands suddenly gripped his ankle, his one intact eye staring up. He plowed a slug into Stanton's chest and the man finally lay still.

McCoy looked at Crooked Finger.

The Indian nodded. He spoke and gestured, and Spur finally understood that they didn't want the body. He smiled and watched the Indians leave.

Stanton lay on the ground motionless. Spur sat under a tree looking at him. He'd never met the man, and now would never know why he was so determined to wipe out the Navajo that he'd hire an army.

After a few minutes he rose, tracked down Stanton's horse but not Colby's, walked her back to the body, which he slumped over the saddle, then tied the man's wrists and ankles together under the horse's belly.

"Makkoi," a soft voice said from several yards away.

Spur turned and watched as an old Indian rode up to him. Chief Eagle Feather sat fairly erect, wrapped in a blanket, on a pony. "He is dead."

"Yes."

"I am glad." He sighed. "He was bad, killed my people, your people. Now he kill no more."

"No," Spur said.

"It is good," Eagle Feather said. "Now I can die in peace."

"What was that?" Spur asked, looking up at the chief.

"Crooked Finger will be new chief," the old man

said, "when I am gone."

"A fine man," Spur said, not knowing whether the Indian understood him or not.

"It is finished in beauty," the chief said.

"Indeed." Spur waved and they parted. Spur headed for Hanging Rocks, leading Stanton on the last ride he'd ever take.

An hour later Spur rode up before the sheriff's office. Hughes burst from inside as McCoy stopped at the hitching post.

"Who is it?" Hughes asked as he peered at the body.

"Michael Stanton. Dave Colby's body is back in the woods somewhere."

"Why the hell you'd shoot them?" Hughes asked. "You better have a goddamned good excuse for this, McCoy!"

"He killed the MacDonalds and the Goodnights. He confessed. I tried to take him alive, and had a scuffle with the Navajo—seems they wanted him."

Hughes' face softened. "What happened?"

"The Indians stuck him full of arrows, and I finished him off."

Hughes shook his head. "I don't see Stanton as a killer."

"Goddamnit, Hughes!" Spur said. "I'm too tired to argue with you. Let's dump Stanton's body and ride out to retrieve Colby's. *Now,* before I'm too tired or pissed at you to do it."

Hughes' face flushed, but he raced into his office, returned with his rifle, and they rode off for the woods.

Spur left the sheriff to haul Colby to the undertaker's. He rode down the street and stopped first

196

at the Stanton house, where his knock brought Caroline to the door.

"Why, Mr. McCoy!" she said happily.

It was the same girl. She was Stanton's daughter. "I have some bad news for you," he said.

Her face was blank. "What news?"

"Your father's dead, Caroline."

She gasped, covered her mouth with a hand and looked away from him.

"I'm sorry," Spur whispered, following her with his eyes as she walked inside.

"How did he die?" Caroline made her way to a chair and sank into it, pressing her feet on the ground and folding her hands.

Spur was silent for a moment.

She looked up at him. "You killed him. Didn't you?"

"Yes and no. The Indians—"

"The Indians!" she said, laughing crazily.

"Let me explain. I'm a government agent here in Hanging Rocks to investigate the deaths of the ranching families killed here about two weeks ago," Spur said quietly. "My investigation led to your father. He'd killed them and several Navajo."

"I see," Caroline said. "Now it all makes sense—somehow."

Spur stood in the doorway, uncertain whether to leave or stay. She glanced up at him sharply.

"Come in."

Spur did so, hat in hand, but left the door open behind him. As he approached her Caroline suddenly rose, disappeared for a moment, then returned with a glass of wine. "I knew something was wrong," she said. "Things haven't been quite right around here. But I didn't know—I didn't know it was anything like this." She sipped the liquid, which made her sneeze.

Spur turned to leave. "I'm sorry," he said again.

"Don't be." Caroline's voice was bitter. "You were only doing your job." Her gaze was palpable.

"Goodbye, Miss Stanton." He walked to the door.

"No, wait; I didn't mean that." She went to him, touched his back. As he turned she smiled. "You did what you had to do. I understand. If my father was guilty if doesn't matter if he died by a bullet, an Indian's arrow, or at the end of a rope. It's all the same in the end."

"What will you do now?" Spur asked, remembering she was eighteen years old.

Before his gaze Caroline's shoulders pushed back, her eyes opened fully and brows lifted, and she looked at Spur. "I have to find someone who knows money and business," she said. "Someone to handle father's affairs. I don't know the first thing about mines or stores or leases, but I'll learn." A smile lit her face. "I'll become a business woman, and I'll be successful at it. After that—I don't know."

"I'm just—"

She shook her head. "Don't say it again, Spur. It doesn't matter. He wasn't my father anymore—he hadn't been for years. Ever since Mother died he's acted strangely, and these last few months have been the worst. I'm mad at myself for not seeing what kind of man he'd become."

"Don't blame yourself," Spur said, and he rubbed her shoulders. "I have to go now, make some more calls."

"Come see me before you go, Spur. Promise me?" Her voice and eyes were full of urgency.

Spur nodded. "I will." He left the house.

Walking to Margaret Bishop's he remembered the new look in Caroline's eyes, and fiery self-determination that should keep her going in her father's absence. He knocked on the screen door at Margaret's. Almost immediately it opened and she stood before him.

"Spur!" she said. "You look terrible!"

"Michael Stanton." He walked in.

"I beg your pardon?" Margaret closed the door and followed him into the parlor, where Spur had slumped into a chair.

"What do you mean, Michael Stanton?"

"Yesterday you asked me who killed Running Bear," he said, exhausted, drowsing. "It was Stanton and Colby."

Margaret looked at him quietly. "Where is he?"

"They're both dead."

She smiled. "Then that's that. It's over. Until I knew who had killed him I didn't believe it; it didn't seem real. Now I can go on."

Spur smiled. "Good. I thought you should know." His chin bobbed as he slipped in and out of consciousness.

"Mr. McCoy, are you all right?"

"Just tired," he said.

"Well, you just rest then," Margaret said.

It was the last thing Spur heard as he nodded off in the chair.

TWENTY-ONE

"Where is the shaman?" Crooked Finger asked as he walked into Chief Eagle Feather's hogan. Bright splotches of colored sand on the dirt floor spoke of recent magical rites the medicine men had been carrying out to save the old man's life.

Eagle Feather gave the barest smile. "I sent him away. I knew those chants before he was born."

"But you will die," the Indian said sadly.

"Yes. We all have to die. I happen to know when."

Crooked Finger looked at him. "When?"

"Tonight." The eyes were not sad as he spoke the word.

The brave gripped his arm gently. "Tonight? But that is so little time."

Chief Eagle Feather nodded. "That is why I have sent for you, Crooked Finger. I have no sons," he said plainly.

Crooked Finger looked away. "Why are you telling me this?"

"Because you shall be chief."

The man gasped. "What?"

"I have decided." He frowned. "Rainbow Dream would have taken my place upon my death by

201

force, had I not killed him." Chief Eagle Feather studied the man's reaction intently.

Crooked Finger looked down, then at him. "Why? Why did you kill Rainbow Dream?"

"He would have destroyed us. That is something you must learn, if you are to be chief: when to fight, and when to avoid fighting."

The brave's eyes rolled. "I do not know what you say, Eagle Feather!"

"You will, in time." He smiled fully. "I have picked well. Lead the *Dine*, the People, to happiness and peace with the white man. Take the best of their ways but preserve the greatest of ours. Only in this way will we have another generation to which we can pass our language, religion, customs—all that makes us the *Dine*. Know these things, Crooked Finger," the elderly chief said, and laid his fist on the man's bare chest. It was still warm from the sun. "Receive the power, my son."

"What do you mean?"

Chief Eagle Feather unclasped his hand and pushed a cactus thron into Crooked Finger's chest. The man didn't scream out as the chief tore his skin down toward his heart. Bright red glowed on his breast.

Eagle Feather chanted an old song, a song about power and lightning and wind, of the gifts of the gods that Crooked Finger would receive, about his strength and bravery, but he didn't concentrate on the words.

He gazed at the young man, who knelt before him confused, bleeding, in pain, but strong. This would be a fine chief. Running Bear would have been better, but he was gone. Crooked Finger would preserve his people.

He sacrificed well, Eagle Feather thought, removing the spine. The chief rubbed its bloodied shaft on Crooked Finger's forehead, cheeks and lips, then halted his chant and threw the spine onto the fire.

"You have sacrificed pain for the gods. Go in power, my friend, *Chief* Crooked Finger."

The Indian rose, blinking against the sudden moisture in his eyes, seemingly oblivious to the hole on his chest which spewed blood as he rose. Drops of red stained his softly worked leather breechcloth. The new chief walked from the hogan in a daze, not looking back.

Eagle Feather smiled and smelled the blood on his fingers. It was finished. The tribe would continue. He shivered as the cold set in again— too early, Eagle Feather thought, then relaxed, into it. He knew it was the chill of the earth, Mother Earth who spread her arms lovingly to welcome him back to her bosom.

The shaman-chief lay calmly as he sensed his body dying, piece by piece, until he felt his soul sucked upward in a rush of wind and then felt no more.

Spur woke as his head hit his chest again. He looked up at Margaret and grinned.

"I'm sorry," he said sheepishly. "Guess I dozed off."

She smiled. "I don't mind. You've had a hard day. Would you like something to eat?"

The idea hit Spur's stomach like a fist. "Haven't eaten all day. That sounds great."

"Would you like anything special? I could fix you something." She looked at him with concerned eyes.

He smiled. "Anything, as long as it's food."

"Fine. And I'll bring the coffee too."

Spur walked with her to the kitchen. "Mind if I

come along?'' he asked.

"Not at all. I thought you might want to rest," she said, and looked over her shoulder.

Spur watched her hips swing back and forth as they went to the kitchen. They were so inviting, packed tightly into Margaret's skirt and petticoats. He felt his weariness vanish. Maybe after dinner, if she wasn't doing anything, they could get to know each other again.

The memories of their bedroom acrobatics sent a tingle through his nervous system. Margaret went straight to the stove, where a pot of coffee simmered, as Spur watched her behind.

"This is just what you need," she said, and splashed it into a china cup.

"Thanks."

As she turned back to the stove, Margaret spilled coffee from the pot. "Darn!" she said, putting the pot down. She took a flour sack towel and bent to wipe the spot.

Spur set his coffee on the counter and walked up behind her, then pressed his groin against her warm bottom.

"Mmmm. That feels wonderful!" Margaret said and pushed back against him.

He fitted his genitals into her cleft and rubbed as Margaret dropped the forgotten cloth but retained her position, sighing.

"We can eat later," Spur said.

"Yes. Oh yes!"

He hiked up her dress and petticoats, exposing her bloomers. Spur pulled them down gently and her soft white bottom blossomed into view. He grunted as he reached down and spread her vaginal lips.

"Spur, I'm hungry too. There. *Right there!*" Margaret gasped.

He rubbed her clit, sending her into convulsions. "No, not so fast," he said. "Last time we did it quick. I think we can slow down now." Spur removed his finger, hoisted her bloomers back up and grasped the woman's shoulders, pulling her up.

"All right, Spur. If that's what you want."

"Maybe I should clean up first?" Spur asked, suddenly aware of the stench from his armpits.

She smiled. "If you want. I could wash you."

"Great idea!"

They put two kettles on to boil and Spur stuffed the firebox of the stove with wood. Margaret then started unbuttoning his shirt.

"Hey!" he said. "The water won't be hot for—"

"I don't care about the water. *I'm* hot." She wrestled the shirt off him, then touched the hairs that curled on his chest, running her fingers through them and lightly digging in her nails. "Running Bear didn't have hair there," she said, and then pushed her face against it. "God, I love the smell of a man!" Her lip brushed past his nipple and up to his neck, where she lapped at his stubble. "And the taste!"

Spur shivered under her administrations. "Margaret, is there anything you won't do or say?"

She laughed. "I figure with what I've done nothing is too much, too shocking. If I'm going to have fun, I'm not holding anything back." She kissed his nose. "Certainly not with you!"

"Glad to hear it."

Margaret ran her hands down his back. "A man's body looks different from a woman's—and I don't mean just this," she said, and pushed her groin against his. Her hands outlined his buttocks. "A man's body is harder, firmer, more powerful."

Spur cupped her behind. "And a woman's is softer, more rounded," he said. "Especially her ass."

"Yes."

The water simmered as they stood before the stove and felt each other. Spur unbuttoned her dress and she slipped out of it. He then gently removed her petticoats and chemise, gasping as he saw her breasts.

"Anything wrong?" she asked.

"No. I just forgot how incredible your tits are. I could suck and fuck them all night, if you'd let me."

Margaret smiled. "But there's so much more. Maybe—half the night."

Spur laughed and squeezed her globes. "It's a deal." He bent and sucked one in, making Margaret shiver. Her nipples hardened under his tongue, and Spur felt his own hardness pound in his pants.

She finished undressing Spur. Margaret even helped him off with his boots.

"I used to do that for my husband, all those years ago." She looked at the kitchen window. "I forgot to close the curtains!" Margaret said.

Spur laughed but his erection danced excitedly before him as he watched her walk naked to the window and pull the blinds closed.

"No one can see us now," she said, and ran back to Spur. "God, you look so good I could eat you up! You're a strong, hairy man and I'm sure as hell glad to be a woman!"

Her eyes made Spur grunt. He lifted her body from the floor, carried her to the bedroom, and threw her onto the mattress.

"Spur!" she said. "What about your bath?"

"Fuck that," he said. "No time. You're so god-

206

damned beautiful!" He laid on top of her. "Hope you don't mind," he said almost apologetically.

"Of course not!" she said. "I was ready to rape you the moment I saw you on my doorstep!" She gripped his thighs with hers powerfully and thrust her groin upward, then chewed on Spur's chin.

"Christ!" he said, and slapped a kiss on her mouth. Spur then moved up until he squatted over her stomach. "Love those tits," Spur said, and bent to lick and suck them individually.

"Eat them!"

Spur felt a hand reach between his legs and grip his testicles, then pulled softly. He slurped her breasts, squeezed and caressed them, did everything he could think to do while Margaret's hands grew bolder and she pulled on his shaft.

"Goddamn!" Spur said, shoving forward. "I want to fuck your tits!" His voice was hoarse.

Margaret squealed with delight and pressed them together, making a tight channel between them. Spur moved up and slid in between them, then pumped into the warm valley as he pinched her nipples.

"Only half the night, remember," Margaret said. She laid her chin on her chest and pushed out her tongue.

Spur felt it touch the head of his penis as he stroked, and so moved up into the warmer target. He pushed into her mouth. Margaret groaned as he entered her and she sucked voraciously on his huge organ. Spur stroked gently to ensure she didn't gag, but she urged him to ram her mouth harder, grabbing his hips and pulled them toward her face.

He felt his control threaten to break, so he eased out of her. Margaret smiled happily and delicately wiped her mouth.

"Mmmm!" she said.

Spur grinned and stretched out over her again. His penis found her hole and he pushed up into her without guiding it, his aim straight and true. Margaret's back arched as his balls banged against her.

"Fuck me, Spur!" she said. "Fuck the breath out of me!"

Margaret bucked as Spur pounded into her, slowly at first, then gradually gaining speed. He suddenly pulled out from her. Margaret nearly screamed.

Spur didn't explain, just flipped her onto her stomach, moved her down until she was bending over the edge of the bed, her arms spread out on the mattress.

He pushed into her from behind, and Margaret sighed as his penis struck her clitoris on the way in. Spur grabbed her hips and pumped quickly, pleasuring Margaret to a quick climax, then another, and finally sending himself over the edge.

Spur shook as he ejaculated. Margaret rammed her hips back against his stomach, forcing his penis deeper into her, sighing and recovering from a third orgasm.

He withdrew from her quickly, turned Margaret over again, and slid back in as they lay on the bed.

After a few moments of silence, their breaths the only sound, Margaret laughed.

"What's so funny?"

"I'm started to feel like a flapjack," Margaret quipped, "the way you kept flipping me."

Spur laughed harshly as he held her. "You complaining?"

"No. But I have ideas too—about ways to do it."

"You'll have to show me sometime," Spur said.

"Not sometime. How about now?"

And she did.